Peter Buchan

Ancient Ballads and Songs of the North of Scotland

Hitherto Unpublished. With Explanatory Notes. Vol. 1

Peter Buchan

Ancient Ballads and Songs of the North of Scotland
Hitherto Unpublished. With Explanatory Notes. Vol. 1

ISBN/EAN: 9783744787147

Printed in Europe, USA, Canada, Australia, Japan

Cover: Foto ©Andreas Hilbeck / pixelio.de

More available books at **www.hansebooks.com**

ANCIENT

BALLADS AND SONGS

OF THE

NORTH OF SCOTLAND,

HITHERTO UNPUBLISHED.

WITH EXPLANATORY NOTES,

BY

PETER BUCHAN,

CORRESPONDING MEMBER OF THE SOCIETY OF ANTIQUARIES OF
SCOTLAND.

" *The ancient spirit is not dead,—*
Old times, we trust, are living here."

Reprinted from the Original Edition of 1828.

VOL. I.

EDINBURGH: WILLIAM PATERSON.
1875.
LL

TO

HIS GRACE

THE

DUKE OF BUCCLEUCH AND QUEENSBERRY,

&c. &c. &c.

My Lord Duke,

I am proud to have the honour of dedicating to your Grace the following Volumes, containing the fruit of many years' painful but pleasant labour :—thus following the example of the late Mr Pinkerton, and the justly-esteemed Sir Walter Scott, who have inscribed their invaluable Collections of Early Song to your Grace's Noble Ancestors.

These Reliques of other years, which have for their object the celebration of the acts of Kings, and the warlike deeds of Heroes, and which so often have cheered the halls, and gladdened the hearts of the good and the brave, will be found, I sincerely trust, worthy of a place among those that have preceded them : for, as their preservation becomes a bounden duty on all true and patriotic Scotsmen, I have gleaned, with pious care, every fragment that could tend to illustrate the History and Antiquities of Scotland; and the Manners, Modes of Living, Religions, and Superstitions of its Inhabitants, as well as their Feelings and Customs, in the fourteenth, fifteenth, sixteenth, and seventeenth centuries.

May your Grace reap that pleasure, on a perusal of these Tales of the Olden Times, which has been experienced by thousands, is the earnest wish of one who has the honour to be,

My Lord Duke,

Your Grace's

Most obedient humble Servant,

PETER BUCHAN.

INTRODUCTION.

In all ages, and by all nations of the world, even in a rude and a barbarous state, has the voice of song been cherished, and made to express the natural feelings of a grateful, a joyful, a brave and a generous heart. Much has been written on the nature and composition of Song, but it all tends to shew that it had its origin in love and gratitude. Love to the Supreme Creator first inspired the muse to tune the heart to sing his praises, and the wonders of indefinite creation, and gratitude continued the song. When man was taught the duties he owed to a Deity, and the obligations he was daily under for his preservation, he testified the same in the fulness of his heart, by the adoration given in his morning and evening songs. Religion and love are synonymous, and expressed in the sweet and delightful cadence of poetical imagery and numbers. When the dawn of nature first began to spread its benign influence over the infant mind of man, and the light of religion dispel the dense mists of heathen darkness, it was like the bursting of a rapid river from its channelled course ; the

longer it ran the wider the breach, and the deeper
the stream the smoother the current.—Such was the
case regarding poetical refinement ; and such was the
happiness of man, when the first rays of light broke
through the dark and almost impenetrable clouds of
ignorance and superstition. Poetical sublimity has
paved the way to the cultivation of man's taste, and
the refinement of his manners and morals. Previous
to the art or discovery of writing and printing, the
religion, the laws, and the histories of times, families,
and particular events, were preserved and handed
down from one generation to another, by a race of
people called Druids, Bards, Scalds, Senachies, Minstrels, &c., who were wont to sing their themes of
religion, love, friendship, war, or history. They were
in great esteem both amongst the Gauls and Britons.
Their function and name doth yet remain among all
those nations which use the old British tongue: and
so much honour was given to them in many places,
that their persons were accounted sacred, and their
houses sanctuaries : nay, in the height of their enmities,
when they managed the cruellest wars one against
another, and used their victories as severely, yet these
Bards and their retinue had free liberty to pass and
repass at their pleasure. The nobles when they
came to them, received them honourably, and dis-
missed them with gifts. They made cantos, and
these not inelegant, which the rhapsodists recited,
either to the better sort, or else to the vulgar, who
were very desirous to hear them; and sometimes they
sung to musical instruments. They were often main-

tained by the chief of the ancient clans, and by some wealthy men, kept on purpose to commemorate their ancestors, and first of their families, in genealogies which they got by heart. In this case, many fly to the Bards and Senachies, as the preservers of ancient records. Tacitus says, that the songs of the German Bards were their only annals. And Joannes Magnus, Archbishop of Upsal, acknowledges, that in compiling the History of the Ancient Goths, he had no other records but the songs of the Bards. As these songs made an illustrious figure at every festival, they were conveyed in every family by parents to their children, and in that manner were kept alive before writing was known. It is to this vanity alone, that we owe the preservation and the remains of ancient poesy.

The Bards made an early appearance in Scotland ; for, "beneath the moss-covered rock of Lona, near his own loud stream, gray in his locks of age, dwells Clonmal, king of harps." They delivered their mysterious doctrines in verses entrusted entirely to memory, which, as a part of their education, their pupils were taught to repeat. They were the oracles, prophets, priests, philosophers, poets, lawgivers, judges, physicians, and teachers of the Gauls ; as their Bards, like the German Scalds, were, more especially, their poets, historians or annalists, and musicians : those communicated their knowledge and precepts also in verse ; and these "sung the battles of heroes, and the heaving bosoms of love." The first traditional records and compositions of all nations were poetical ; and that verse, from custom, was continued, as most impressive and memorable, on subjects thought worthy of preservation. America has ; Asia, Greece, and Italy had their Bards, as well as Gaul ; and the Scalds of the North were equally honoured and famous in Germany. And till of late, there were itinerant Bards, or strolling Minstrels, who performed upon harps, and sung and recited heroic and other ballads. To these rural Minstrels, I am convinced, we are indebted for the preservation of many of our fine old ballads and songs ; many of which will be found to enrich this Collection, culled with the greatest industry and care from among the sons and daughters of the North.

Poetry has been long and justly esteemed as the noblest ebullition of the human soul. Its uses are as various as its power is unbounded ; and let not the vulgar mind ridicule and abuse its votaries as troublesome and useless members of society. But I speak not to those whose faculties are contracted within the narrow sphere of sordid gain ; but to those whose ideas are extended, whose minds are refined, and who can cultivate a taste for polite literature amid the more weighty concerns of business. In the first ages, poetry was generally used to perpetuate the memory of some great event, to sing the praises of heroes, and to honour the remains of those who fell in battle. Some nations (as the Arabians do at present) distinguished the various genealogies of their tribes and families in verse, which was conveyed from father to child as a sort of patrimony. The ideas of the ancient Bards were generally simple and sublime, and ex-

pressed in language at once natural, nervous and fiery;
every sentiment sprung from real feeling, and every
word (such was their conciseness) seemed indispens-
ably necessary to the harmony of the whole.   And,
although many of these bards, or minstrels, were both
untutored and unlettered, their songs are the language
of the heart, and speak the sentiments of the soul, in
familiar verse.

It becomes us then, as the advocates of a national
concern, not to weary in this honoured labour of love;
but to strain every nerve, to preserve from the fast
decaying hand of time, a remnant of those wild flowers
which have garnished the antique halls of an ancient
race of warriors, now long forgotten except in the
sweet voice of magic song.   And, although much has
been done, still much remains undone, in collecting
those mutilated fragments of our early ancestors;—
those graphic relics of antiquity, which delineate men
and manners, kings and heroes, things natural and
supernatural, not as they exist now, but as they were
once believed to be.   It must therefore be gratifying
to every liberal-minded man of taste, and every lover
of his country, to find there are still labourers who
delight to glean in the vineyard of traditionary song,
and snatch from the beds of oblivion, what have at
one time contributed to the greatness of kings, the
pleasures of the commons, the inspiration of heroes,
and been the wonder and delight of ages.   Even to
the man of letters, as well as the literary antiquary,
they become interesting.

No one has yet conceived, nor has it entered the

mind of man, what patience, perseverance, and general
knowledge are necessary for an editor of a Collection
of Ancient Ballads; nor what mountains of difficulties
he has to overcome ; what hosts of enemies he has to
encounter ; and what myriads of little-minded quib-
blers he has to silence.   The writing of explanatory
notes is like no other species of literature.   History
throws little light upon their origin, or the cause
which gave rise to' their composition. He has to
grope his way in the dark ; like Bunyan's pilgrim, on
crossing the valley of the shadow of death, he hears
sounds and noises, but cannot, to a certainty, tell from
whence they come, nor to what place they proceed.
The one time, he has to treat of fabulous ballads in
the most romantic shape; the next legendary, with
all its exploded, obsolete, and forgotten superstitions;
also history, tragedy, comedy, love, war, and so on;
all, perhaps, within the narrow compass of a few
hours,—so varied must his genius and talents be.

The Ballads themselves are faithfully and honestly
transcribed, and given'as taken down from the mouths
of the reciters : they have suffered no change since
they fortunately were consigned to me by their foster
parents.   There are many of them, however, much
like those already published, but under different
names : of these I have been careful to advise my
reader ; also, when and where I have found such likeness.   From such proceedings, it will then be seen
that I have acted as candid and upright a part as
within the compass of the power of any one situated
under similar circumstances.   I have spared neither

money nor trouble, in procuring the most genuine
and best authenticated copies of all the Ancient
Ballads in the following pages, and flatter myself
I have succeeded beyond any of my cotemporaries.
I have also been able to complete many of the very
best pieces hitherto only found in mutilated fragments, even in popular and esteemed collections ;
and trust they will form a valuable acquisition to the
libraries of all those interested in the history of
Scottish literature.   But, as perfection has not yet
been the lot of man, no one will expect that such a
work as this can be altogether free of faults, and
that it is impossible to please every reader : as this
is the case, my great ambition is to gratify those of
a kindred spirit, whose ears are ever open to the re-
cital of the tales of other years ; of their country and
its inhabitants, their loves and wars, joys and woes,
as depicted by worthies, who once, like themselves,
filled an honourable situation in life ; who shared in
the festivities of their day ; but who are now, unless
in the songs of their mirth and sadness, exploded
from the memories of a forgetful world.   Yet a remnant shall be saved ; the lovers of Ancient Minstrels
will find many of those ditties that gladdened the
hearts of their ancestors, and cheered the warlike
halls of their ancient and noble possessors, to enrich
the work now before them.   Although the labourers
in this field of traditionary song have, of late,
proved abundant, and their gleanings made with
pious care, their works will show how thin their
harvest has been.   And, I may add, every year is

making it more and more so, by the demise of some
worthy matron, or hoary-headed sire, who is silently
sliding away at the command of ruthless death, to
where the sons of the morning sing together in
endless concert. There are still, though now few,
some beautiful and sweet morsels of the olden times,
to be found among the aged and venerated people of
the North, that have escaped the most diligent researches of these modern reapers. As much of our
traditionary history, particularly local, is blended
with the family exploits of the times, as recorded
in the olden ballads, their preservation becomes
necessary, and a profitable source of useful informa-
tion and delight, not only to the antiquary, but to
every one who feels an interest in the decayed
memories of their forefathers—who wish to cherish a
national spirit, and who are anxious to support the
time-worn structure, and falling towers of Ancient
Scottish National Song. Let them then rouse each
latent feeling, and encourage those who make such
studies their delight, and who take pleasure in pre-
serving them.

As man has a thinking principle within him, he
is conscious that nothing in this world can perfect
his happiness, so that he flies from one object to
another, with a view of lessening his misery, or in-
creasing his pleasure ; and, as times and ages change,
so do his manners, feeling, and dispositions ; what
was his joy to-day, may become his sorrow to-morrow.
He has at length discovered, that, in recovering the
vestiges of the *olden times*, he anticipates a mental

satisfaction rarely arising from the pursuits of vice. The literature of past ages has engrossed the study and attention of almost every civilized and learned man. He can judge from the works of imagination, the state of the minds of his ancestors, and the manners, and characters of a rude, or an enlightened people, in their native colour and dress. And, as of late years, there has been more than an ordinary enquiry after the poetical reliques of our early history, much has been preserved from the wreck of ages— old things have become new, and a renovation of our Scottish literature seems to have taken place in all the plenitude of its strength and beauty. The darksome ages that gave birth to the mental achievements of our forefathers, are now forgot ; and that spirit only which lay sleeping in the tomb of forgetfulness, arises with the vigour it was wont to show in its chivalric deeds : And, although the age of knight-errantry and chivalry have passed entirely away, those emotions of heroic feeling are still alive in the breasts of many. The human heart still retains the same sentiments of honour, and the lofty magnanimity of the glory of past ages.

To these kindred spirits, do I then offer the pride of my toils ;—the only legitimate history of the superstitions and times in which they were conceived. In them, the lives and actions of kings, nobles, and commons, will be found delineated with the artless and unassuming pen of nature : their ancestors pourtrayed in their true colours, and a display of those deeds which gave rise to their first ambition and greatness. Should, then, the following volumes meet with that encouragement which I anticipate, I will not eat the bread of idleness, but still persevere in culling and garnering up for the sons of Scotsmen yet unborn, those sweetly variegated blossoms which bloom in the straw-covered cot, among the silvery-headed monuments of living antiquity, in the North of my native Isle.

Long, and perhaps tiresome, as this Introduction has been to many of my readers, I must still add a few words more, partly by way of shewing my fervent gratitude, and partly by way of explanation of what follows.—In the first place, it is necessary to say by what means I became possessed of so many valuable reliques as adorn the following pages, as some of my sceptical readers may think them forgeries; but as it is impossible for me to satisfy every person, I must adopt the shortest method, by saying, that the greater part of them was taken down by myself during the last ten or twelve years, from the singing and recitation of old men and women, in various parts of Scotland, but chiefly in Aberdeenshire: others were sent me by ladies and gentlemen of the highest respectability, on whose words, as to their authenticity, I could safely depend; but as it would be too tedious to name them all, although to all my thanks are due, I shall only particularize Hugh Irvine, Esq. Drum; Malvina, a young lady in Aberdeen; and Mr James Nicol, Strichen. I must also mention that I was much indebted to the recitation of James

Rankin, an old man, blind from his birth, with a
most retentive memory, and who is at this moment
gathering for me what can be gleaned within the circle
of a large and extensive acquaintance; as it is my most
earnest wish, and greatest pleasure, to preserve every
fragment and literary monument of our early ancestors, that can illustrate the history and times in
which they had their existence on this terrestrial ball,
however much and unjustly I may be reprobated, as
of late I have been, by ignorant persons, under a false
show of modesty and grace. And, although this is
the first attempt of the kind that was ever made in
the North, I trust it will not be the last; for among
our heath-clad hills the roses as well as the thistles
grow—in the glens, sprigs of the willow are to be
found, and the harp of Apollo often heard !

My best acknowledgments are not less due to John
Richardson, Esq. of Pitfour, Pitfour Castle, Perth-
shire, for the loan of a curious and interesting old
MS. volume of Poems. On the first page of this MS.
is written—" This Buick perteens to a verie honourable womane, Margarat Robertsoune, relict of vm-
quhile Alexander Steuart of Bonskeid, Anno Domini
1630." I am informed she belonged to the Lude
family, and the Poems are those referred to by
General Stewart of Garth, in his sketches of the
Highlands, as containing proofs of the advanced state
of literature in the Highlands in the 17th century.
Of this collection I intended to have given freely ;
but on arriving at Edinburgh, I found the work so
far advanced in the printing as to prevent me from

giving more than two pieces as a specimen, which will be found at the end of this Introduction. However, in a forthcoming volume, which has already been called for, as my Ballad-store is not yet exhausted, I will then avail myself of its contents, and draw upon it largely.

I shall now close this Introduction by observing, that, among the many gentlemen of rank and respectability, who have interested themselves not a little in the success of this publication, am I indebted to Charles Kirkpatrick Sharpe, Esquire, Edinburgh, and to whom I beg to offer, with every sense of respect and esteem, my most sincere thanks for the trouble he has taken in revising the proof-sheets of the Ballads as they emanated from the press, as my living at such a distance from Edinburgh prevented my own corrections. No one, however, that knows the refined taste and superior judgment of this gentleman, in every thing connected with Ancient Scottish Literature, will regret my absence. The Introduction and Notes are as they came from my pen. A tribute of grateful respect is also due to all those who have encouraged the work by their friendly patronage, as without patrons all my labours would have been lost.

To avoid the imputation of vanity, I am anxious to state, that the Portrait prefixed to this volume has been given at the special request of some of my friends in Edinburgh, who have taken an interest in the publication.

PETER BUCHAN.

PETERHEAD, *October* 1828.

ITS A VONDER TO SEE HOW THIS VORLD DOES GOE.

Sumtyme have I sein whein the vorld hes bein mirrie,
    Accepted with melancholly, bot now its grown sad :
Sumtyme have I sein whein the vorld not bein wearie,
    What toyll, or vhat travell, vhat cross we have had.
Now sighing for singing, our mynd is confused,
Now laughing for louing, we loath that we loued ;
Rejoycing, reposing, nothing bot in woe,
Its a vonder to sie how this vorld does goe.

The planets ar changed thair contrary cours,
    And he that vas heighest is lowest broght down ;
And he who was vorthiest now is grown vorst,
    Marc Venus and Mercurie zeild to the Mone.
The Heavins had a hermon, but now is grown heirs,
In mouing thair mover, and chainging ther vers ;
Such chainges, too strainges, as Neptune doe,
Its a vonder to sie how yis vorld does goe.

Now Fortoun turns mad, and Venus a wich,
    Blind Cupid, that fondling, knows not quhair he flies ;
Ther is noe man respectit, bot he that (is) riche,
    True waillour and vertue ar sucken in the skyes.
The gallants ar gayest that gritest can glut,
The follow is fynest that veirs the Frence hat ;
Goe fatlands for hatbands, and shaikers also,
Its a vonder to sie how this vorld doth goe.

The sillie puir peddleris that liuis on ther packs,
    Ar loupen to lordschipes, and lives on ther reut ;
Now gallants and greit men ar all gone aback,
    They clap al in catiourie for skiprigs yai spent.
Now he (is) ane lord that lait was ane cloun,
And she is ane ladey that lait was a loun,
Cum hurly, cum burly, the vsurer so,
    Its a vounder to sie how this vorld doth goe.

JAMES HERUIE.

My love band me with a kisse,
  Yat I sould no langer stay ;
Quhen I felt so sweit a blisse,
  I had les pourer to pairt away ;
Allace yat woman doth not know,
Kisses mak men loth to goe !

Zes, she knawes it bot too weil,
  For I hard when Venus doue,
In her eares did softlie tell,
  Yat kisses were the sealles of loue ;
Och much not then though it be so,
Kisses mak men loth to go !

Wherfor did she thus inflame,
  My desyres heats my blood ;
Instantlye to quenche the same,
  And sterue whom she had given foode ;
I, I, ye comming sence can sho,
Kisses mak men loth to goe !

Had she bid me goe at first,
  It wald neer haue greud my hairt ;
Hoop delayd had bein worst,
  But och to kisse, and then to pairt ;
How deip it strock, speak, gods, you kno,
Kisses mak men loth to go !

CONTENTS.

VOL. I.   B

ANCIENT

BALLADS AND SONGS

OF THE

NORTH OF SCOTLAND.

Sir Patrick Spens.

THE King sits in Dunfermline town,
　A' drinking at the wine ;
Says, Where will I get a good skipper
　Will sail the saut seas fine ?

Out it speaks an eldren knight
　Amang the companie,—
Young Patrick Spens is the best skipper
　That ever sail'd the sea.

The king he wrote a braid letter,
　And seal'd it wi' his ring ;
Says, Ye'll gi'e that to Patrick Spens,
　See if ye can him find.

He sent this, not wi' an auld man,
   Nor yet a simple boy,
But the best o' nobles in his train
   This letter did convoy.

When Patrick look'd the letter upon
   A light laugh then ga'e he;
But ere he read it till an end,
   The tear blinded his e'e.

Ye'll eat and drink, my merry men a',
   An' see ye be weell thorn;
For blaw it weet, or blaw it wind,
   My guid ship sails the morn.

Then out it speaks a guid auld man,
   A guid death mat he dee,—
Whatever ye do, my guid master,
   Tak' God your guide to bee.

For late yestreen I saw the new moon,
   The auld moon in her arm.
Ohon, alas! says Patrick Spens,
   That bodes a deadly storm.

But I maun sail the seas the morn,
   And likewise sae maun you;
To Noroway, wi' our king's daughter,—
   A chosen queen she's now.

But I wonder who has been sae base,
 As tauld the king o' mee :
Even tho' hee ware my ae brither,
 An ill death mat he dee.

Now Patrick he rigg'd out his ship,
 And sailed ower the faem ;
But mony a dreary thought had hee,
 While hee was on the main.

They hadna sail'd upon the sea
 A day but barely three ;
Till they came in sight o' Noroway,
 It's there where they must bee.

They hadna stayed into that place
 A month but and a day,
Till he caus'd the flip in mugs gae roun',
 And wine in cans sae gay ;

The pipe and harp sae sweetly play'd,
 The trumpets loudly soun' ;
In every hall where in they stay'd,
 Wi' their mirth did reboun'.

Then out it speaks an auld skipper,
 An inbearing dog was hee,—
Ye've stay'd ower lang in Noroway,
 Spending your king's monie.

Then out it speaks Sir Patrick Spens,—
  O how can a' this bee ?
I ha'e a bow o' guid red gowd
  Into my ship wi' mee.

But betide me well, betide me wae,
  This day I'se leave the shore ;
And never spend my king's monie
  'Mong Noroway dogs no more.

Young Patrick hee is on the sea,
  And even on the faem ;
Wi' five-an-fifty Scots lords' sons,
  That lang'd to bee at hame.

They hadna sail'd upon the sea
  A day but barely three ;
Till loud and boistrous grew the wind,
  And stormy grew the sea.

O where will I get a little wee boy
  Will tak' my helm in hand,
Till I gae up to my tapmast
  And see for some dry land ?

He hadna gane to his tapmast
  A step but barely three ;
Ere thro' and thro' the bonny ship's side,
  He saw the green haw-sea.

There are five-an-fifty feather beds
   Well packed in ae room ;
And ye'll get as muckle guid canvas
   As wrap the ship a' roun' ;

Ye'll pict her well, and spare her not,
   And mak' her hale and soun'.
But ere he had the word well spoke
   The bonny ship was down.

O laith, laith were our guid lords' sons
   To weet their milk-white hands ;
But lang ere a' the play was ower
   They wat their gowden bands.

O laith, laith were our Scots lords' sons
   To weet their coal-black shoon ;
But lang ere a' the play was ower
   They wat their hats aboon.

It's even ower by Aberdour
   It's fifty fathoms deep,
And yonder lies Sir Patrick Spens,
   And a's men at his feet.

It's even ower by Aberdour,
   There's mony a craig and fin,
And yonder lies Sir Patrick Spens,
   Wi' mony a guid lord's son.

Lang, lang will the ladyes look
   Into their morning weed,
Before they see young Patrick Spens
   Come sailing ower the fleed.

Lang, lang will the ladyes look
   Wi' their fans in their hand,
Before they see him, Patrick Spens,
   Come sailing to dry land.

Young Akin.

Lady Margaret sits in her bower door
   Sewing at her silken seam;
She heard a note in Elmond's-wood,
   And wish'd she there had been.

She loot the seam fa' frae her side,
   And the needle to her tae;
And she is on to Elmond's-wood
   As fast as she cou'd gae.

She hadna pu'd a nut, a nut,
   Nor broken a branch but ane,
Till by it came a young hind chiel,
   Says, Lady lat alane.

O why pu' ye the nut, the nut,
  Or why brake ye the tree;
For I am forester o' this wood,
  Ye shou'd spier leave at me?

I'll ask leave at no living man,
  Nor yet will I at thee;
My father is king o'er a' this realm,
  This wood belongs to me.

She hadna pu'd a nut, a nut,
  Nor broken a branch but three,
Till by it came him young Akin,
  And gar'd her lat them be.

The highest tree in Elmond's-wood,
  He's pu'd it by the reet;
And he has built for her a bower
  Near by a hallow seat.

He's built a bower, made it secure
  Wi' carbuncle and stane;
Tho' travellers were never sae nigh
  Appearance it had nane.

He's kept her there in Elmond's-wood,
  For six lang years and one;
Till six pretty sons to him she bear,
  And the seventh she's brought home.

It fell ance upon a day,
 This guid lord went from home ;
And he is to the hunting gane,
 Took wi' him his eldest son.

And when they were on a guid way,
 Wi' slowly pace did walk ;
The boy's heart being something wae,
 He thus began to talk :—

A question I wou'd ask, father,
 Gin ye wou'dna angry be.
Say on, say on, my bonny boy,
 Ye'se nae be quarrell'd by me.

I see my mither's cheeks aye weet,
 I never can see them dry ;
And I wonder what aileth my mither
 To mourn continually.

Your mither was a king's daughter,
 Sprung frae a high degree ;
And she might ha'e wed some worthy prince,
 Had she nae been stown by me ;

I was her father's cup-bearer,
 Just at that fatal time ;
I catch'd her on a misty night,
 Whan summer was in prime ;

My luve to her was most sincere,
　Her luve was great for me ;
But when she hardships doth endure,
　Her folly she does see.

I'll shoot the buntin' o' the bush,
　The linnet o' the tree,
And bring them to my dear mither,
　See if she'll merrier be.

It fell upo' another day,
　This guid lord he thought lang,
And he is to the hunting gane,
　Took wi' him his dog and gun ;

Wi' bow and arrow by his side,
　He's aff, single, alane ;
And left his seven children to stay
　Wi' their mither at hame.

O, I will tell to you, mither,
　Gin ye wadna angry be.
Speak on, speak on, my little wee boy,
　Ye'se nae be quarrell'd by me.

As we came frae the hynd hunting,
　We heard fine music ring.
My blessings on you, my bonny boy,
　I wish I'd been there my lane.

He's ta'en his mither by the hand,
   His six brithers also,
And they are on thro' Elmond's-wood,
   As fast as they cou'd go ;

They wistna weel where they were gaen,
   Wi' the stratlins o' their feet ;
They wistna weel where they were gaen
   Till at her father's yate.

I hae nae money in my pocket,
   But royal rings hae three ;
I'll gie them you, my little young son,
   And ye'll walk there for me ;

Ye'll gi'e the first to the proud porter,
   And he will lat you in ;
Ye'll gi'e the next to the butler boy,
   And he will show you ben ;

Ye'll gi'e the third to the minstrel
   That plays before the king ;
He'll play success to the bonny boy,
   Came thro' the wood him lane.

He ga'e the first to the proud porter,
   And he open'd an' let him in ;
He ga'e the next to the butler boy,
   And he has shown him ben ;

He ga'e the third to the minstrel
   That play'd before the king ;
And he play'd success to the bonny boy
   Came thro' the wood him lane.

Now when he came before the king,
   Fell low down on his knee ;
The king he turned round about,
   And the saut tear blinded his ee.

Win up, win up, my bonny boy,
   Gang frae my companie ;
Ye look sae like my dear daughter,
   My heart will birst in three.

If I look like your dear daughter,
   A wonder it is none ;
If I look like your dear daughter,—
   I am her eldest son.

Will ye tell me, ye little wee boy,
   Where may my Margaret be ?
She's just now standing at your yates,
   And my six brithers her wi'.

O where are all my porter boys
   That I pay meat and fee,
To open my yates baith wide and braid ?
   Let her come in to me.

When she came in before the king,
  Fell low down on her knee :
Win up, win up, my daughter dear,
  This day ye'll dine wi' me.

Ae bit I canno' eat, father,
  Nor ae drop can I drink,
Till I see my mither and sister dear
  For lang for them I think.

When she came before the queen,
  Fell low down on her knee :
Win up, win up, my daughter dear,
  This day ye'se dine wi' me.

Ae bit I canno' eat, mither,
  Nor ae drop can I drink,
Until I see my dear sister,
  For lang for her I think.

When that these two sisters met,
  She hail'd her courteouslie :
Come ben, come ben, my sister dear,
  This day ye'se dine wi' me.

Ae bit I canno' eat, sister,
  Nor ae drop can I drink,
Until I see my dear husband,
  For lang for him I think.

O where are all my rangers bold,
   That I pay meat and fee,
To search the forest far an' wide,
   And bring Akin to me?

Out it speaks the little wee boy,—
   Na, na, this maunna be ;
Without ye grant a free pardon,
   I hope ye'll nae him see.

O here I grant a free pardon,
   Well seal'd by my own han' ;
Ye may make search for young Akin,
   As soon as ever you can.

They search'd the country wide and braid,
   The forests far and near ;
And found him into Elmond's-wood,
   Tearing his yellow hair.

Win up, win up, now young Akin,
   Win up and boun wi' me ;
We're messengers come from the court,
   The king wants you to see.

O lat him take frae me my head,
   Or hang me on a tree ;
For since I've lost my dear lady,
   Life's no pleasure to me.

Your head will nae be touch'd, Akin,
    Nor hang'd upon a tree ;
Your lady's in her father's court,
    And all he wants is thee.

When he came in before the king,
    Fell low down on his knee.
Win up, win up, now young Akin,
    This day ye'se dine wi' me.

But as they were at dinner set,
    The boy asked a boun ;
I wish we were in the good church,
    For to get Christendoun ;

We ha'e lived in guid green wood
    This seven years and ane ;
But a' this time since e'er I mind,
    Was never a church within.

Your asking's nae sae great, my boy,
    But granted it shall be ;
This day to guid church ye shall gang,
    And your mither shall gang you wi'.

When unto the guid church she came,
    She at the door did stan' ;
She was sae sair sunk down wi' shame,
    She cou'dna come farer ben.

Then out it speaks the parish priest,
  And a sweet smile gae he ;
Come ben, come ben, my lily flower,
  Present your babes to me.

Charles, Vincent, Sam, and Dick,
  And likewise James and John ;
They call'd the eldest Young Akin,
  Which was his father's name.

Then they staid in the royal court,
  And liv'd wi' mirth and glee ;
And when her father was deceas'd,
  Heir of the crown was she.

Young Waters.

It fell about the good Yule time
  When caps and stoups gaed roun' ;
Down it came him young Waters,
  To welcome James, our king.

The great, the great, rade a' together ;
  The sma' came a' behin' ;
But wi' young Waters, that brave knight,
  There came a gay gatherin'.

The horse young Waters rade upon,
   It cost him hunders nine ;
For he was siller shod before,
   And gowd graith had behin' ;

At ilka tippit o' his horse mane
   There hang a siller bell ;
The wind was loud, the steed was proud,
   And they gae a sindry knell.

The king he lay ower's castle wa',
   Beheld baith dale and down ;
And he beheld him, young Waters,
   Come riding to the town.

He turn'd him right and round about,
   And to the queen said he,—
Who is the bravest man, my dame,
   That ever your een did see ?

I've seen lairds, and I've seen lords,
   And knights o' high degree ;
But a braver man than young Waters
   My een did never see.

He turn'd him right and roun' about,
   And ane angry man was he ;
O wae to you, my dame, the queen,
   Ye might ha'e excepted me !

Ye are nae laird, ye are nae lord,
    Ye are the king that wears the crown ;
There's nae a lord in fair Scotland,
    But unto you maun a' bow down.

O, lady, for your love choicing,
    Ye shall win to your will ;
The morn, or I eat or drink,
    Young Waters I'll gar kill.

And nevertheless, the king cou'd say,
    Ye might ha'e excepted me ;
Yea for yea, the king cou'd say,
    Young Waters he shall die.

Likewise for your ill-wyled words,
    Ye sall ha'e cause to mourn ;
Gin ye hadna been sae big wi' child,
    Ye on a hill su'd burn.

Young Waters came before the king,
    Fell low down on his knee ;
Win up, win up, young Waters,
    What's this I hear o' thee ?

What ails the king at me, he said,
    What ails the king at me ?
It is tauld me the day, sir knight,
    Ye've done me treasonie.

Liars will lie on fell gude men,
  Sae will they do on me ;
I wudna wish to be the man
  That liars on wudna lie.

Nevertheless, the king cou'd say,
  In prison strang gang ye ;
O yea for yea, the king cou'd say,
  Young Waters ye shall die.

Syne they ha'e ta'en him, young Waters,
  Laid him in prison strang ;
And left him there wi' fetters boun',
  Making a heavy mane.

Aft ha'e I ridden thro' Striveling town,
  Thro' heavy wind and weet ;
But ne'er rade I thro' Striveling town
  Wi' fetters on my feet.

Aft ha'e I ridden thro' Striveling town
  Thro' heavy wind and rain ;
But ne'er rade I thro' Striveling town,
  But thought to ridden't again.

They brought him to the heading hill,
  His horse, bot and his saddle ;
And they brought to the heading hill,
  His young son in his cradle.

And they brought to the heading hill,
 His hounds intill a leish ;
And they brought till the heading hill,
 His gos-hawk in a jess.

King James he then rade up the hill,
 And mony a man him wi' ;
And called on his trusty page,
 To come right speedilie.

Ye'll do' ye to the Earl o' Mar,
 For he sits on yon hill ;
Bid him loose the brand frae his bodie,
 Young Waters for to kill.

O gude forbid, the Earl he said,
 The like su'd e'er fa' me ;
My body e'er su'd wear the brand,
 That gars young Waters die.

Then he has loos'd his trusty brand,
 And casten't in the sea :
Says, Never lat them get a brand,
 Till it come back to me.

The scaffold it prepared was,
 And he did mount it hie ;
And a' spectators that were there,
 The saut tears blint their e'e.

O had your tongues, my brethren dear,
    And mourn nae mair for me ;
Ye're seeking grace frae a graceless face,
    For there is nane to gie.

Ye'll tak' a bit o' canvas claith,
    And put it ower my ee ;
And Jack, my man, ye'll be at hand,
    The hour that I su'd die.

Syne aff ye'll tak' my bluidy sark,
    Gie it fair Margaret Grahame ;
For she may curse the dowie dell
    That brought King James, him hame.

Ye'll bid her mak' her bed narrow,
    And mak' it naeways wide ;
For a braver man than young Waters
    Will ne'er streek by her side.

Bid her do weel to my young son,
    And gie him nurses three ;
For gin he live to be a man,
    King James will gar him die.

He call'd upon the headsman, then,
    A purse o' gowd him gae ;
Says, Do your office, headsman, boy,
    And mak' nae mair delay.

O head me soon, O head me clean,
  And pit me out o' pine ;
For it is by the king's command,—
  Gang head me till his min'.

Tho' by him I'm condemn'd to die,
  I'm lieve to his ain kin ;
And for the truth, I'll plainly tell,
  I am his sister's son.

Gin ye're my sister's son, he said,
  It is unkent to me.
O mindna ye on your sister, Bess,
  That lives in the French countrie ?

Gin Bess then be your mither dear,
  As I trust well she be ;
Gae hame, gae hame, young Waters,
  Ye'se ne'er be slain by me.

But he lay by his napkin fine,
  Was saft as ony silk ;
And on the block he laid his neck,
  Was whiter than the milk.

Says, Strike the blow, ye headsman boy,
  And that right speedilie ;
It's never be said here gaes a knight,
  Was ance condemn'd to die.

The head was ta'en frae young Waters,
   And mony tears for him shed;
But mair did mourn for fair Margaret,
   As raving, she lyes mad.

The Gowans sae Gay.

Fair lady Isabel sits in her bower sewing,
   Aye as the gowans grow gay;
There she heard an elf-knight blawing his horn,
   The first morning in May.

If I had yon horn that I hear blawing.
   Aye as the gowans grow gay;
And yon elf-knight to sleep in my bosom,
   The first morning in May.

This maiden had scarcely these words spoken,
   Aye as the gowans grow gay;
Till in at her window the elf-knight has luppen, ⸝
   The first morning in May.

Its a very strange matter, fair maiden, said he,
   Aye as the gowans grow gay,
I canna' blaw my horn, but ye call on me,
   The first morning in May.

But will ye go to yon greenwood side,
  Aye as the gowans grow gay?
If ye canna' gang, I will cause you to ride,
  The first morning in May.

He leapt on a horse, and she on another,
  Aye as the gowans grow gay;
And they rode on to the greenwood together,
  The first morning in May.

Light down, light down, lady Isabel, said he,
  Aye as the gowans grow gay;
We are come to the place where ye are to die,
  The first morning in May.

Ha'e mercy, ha'e mercy, kind sir, on me,
  Aye as the gowans grow gay;
Till ance my dear father and mother I see,
  The first morning in May.

Seven kings' daughters here hae I slain,
  Aye as the gowans grow gay;
And ye shall be the eight o' them,
  The first morning in May. ·

O sit down a while, lay your head on my knee,
  Aye as the gowans grow gay;
That we may hae some rest before that I die,
  The first morning in May.

She stroak'd him sae fast, the nearer he did creep,
   Aye as the gowans grow gay;
Wi' a sma' charm she lull'd him fast asleep,
   The first morning in May.

Wi' his ain sword belt sae fast as she ban' him,
   Aye as the gowans grow gay;
Wi' his ain dag-durk sae sair as she dang him,
   The first morning in May.

If seven kings' daughters here ye ha'e slain,
   Aye as the gowans grow gay,
Lye ye here, a husband to them a',
   The first morning in May.

The Twa Magicians.

The lady stands in her bower door,
   As straight as willow wand;
The blacksmith stood a little forebye,
   Wi' hammer in his hand.

Weel may ye dress ye, lady fair,
   Into your robes o' red,
Before the morn at this same time,
   I'll gain your maidenhead.

Awa', awa', ye coal-black-smith,
   Wou'd ye do me the wrang,
To think to gain my maidenhead,
   That I hae kept sae lang.

Then she has hadden up her hand,
   And she sware by the mold,
I wu'dna be a blacksmith's wife,
   For the full o' a chest o' gold.

I'd rather I were dead and gone,
   And my body laid in grave,
Ere a rusty stock o' coal-black-smith,
   My maidenhead shou'd have.

But he has hadden up his hand,
   And he sware by the mass,
I'll cause ye be my light leman,
   For the hauf o' that and less.
Chorus.—O bide, lady, bide,
      And he bade her bide ;
      The rusty smith your leman shall be,
         For a' your muckle pride.

Then she became a turtle dow,
   To fly up in the air ;
And he became another dow,
   And they flew pair and pair.
         O bide, lady, bide, &c.

She turn'd hersell into an eel,
    To swim into yon burn ;
And he became a speckled trout,
    To gie the eel a turn.
        O bide, lady, bide, &c.

Then she became a duck, a duck,
    To puddle in a peel ;
And he became a rose-kaim'd drake,
    To gie the duck a dreel.
        O bide, lady, bide, &c.

She turn'd hersell into a hare,
    To rin upon yon hill ;
And he became a gude grey hound,
    And boldly he did fill.
        O bide, lady, bide, &c.

Then she became a gay grey mare,
    And stood in yonder slack ;
And he became a gilt saddle,
    And sat upon her back.
Chorus.—Was she wae, he held her sae,
        And still he bade her bide ;
        The rusty-smith her leman was,
        For a' her muckle pride.

Then she became a het girdle,
    And he became a cake ;

And a' the ways she turn'd hersell,
    The blacksmith was her make.
        Was she wae, &c.

She turn'd hersell into a ship,
    To sail out ower the flood ;
He ca'ed a nail intill her tail,
    And syne the ship she stood.
        Was she wae, &c.

Then she became a silken plaid,
    And stretch'd upon a bed ;
And he became a green covering,
    And gain'd her maiden-head.
Chorus.—Was she wae, he held her sae,
        And still he bade her bide ;
        The rusty smith her leman was,
        For a' her muckle pride.

Childe Owlet.

Lady Erskine sits in her chamber,
    Sewing at her silken seam,
A chain of gold for Childe Owlet,
    As he goes out and in.

But it fell ance upon a day,
  She unto him did say ;
Ye must cuckold Lord Ronald,
  For a' his lands and ley.

O cease, forbid, Madam, he says,
  That this shou'd e'er be done ;
How would I cuckold Lord Ronald,
  And me his sister's son ?

Then she's ta'en out a little penknife,
  That lay below her bed ;
Put it below her green stay's cord,
  Which made her body bleed.

Then in it came him, Lord Ronald,
  Hearing his lady's moan ;
What blood is this, my dear, he says,
  That sparks on the fire stone ?

Young Childe Owlet, your sister's son.
  Is now gane frae my bower ;
If I hadna been a good woman,
  I'd been Childe Owlet's whore.

Then he has ta'en him, Childe Owlet,
  Laid him in prison strong ;
And all his men a council held,
  How they wou'd work him wrong.

Some said, they wou'd Childe Owlet hang ;
   Some said they wou'd him burn ;
Some said they wou'd have Childe Owlet
   Between wild horses torn.

There are horses in your stables stand,
   Can run right speedilie ;
And ye will to your stable go,
   And wile out four for me.

They put a foal to ilka foot,
   And ane to ilka hand ;
And sent them down to Darling muir,
   As fast as they cou'd gang.

There was not a kow in Darling muir,
   Nor ae piece o' a rind,
But drappit o' Childe Owlet's blude,
   And pieces o' his skin.

There was not a kow in Darling muir,
   Nor ae piece o' a rash ;
But drappit o' Childe Owlet's blude,
   And pieces o' his flesh.

The Bent sae Brown.

There are sixteen lang miles I'm sure,
    Between my love and me ;
There are eight o' them in gude dry land.
    And other eight by sea.

Betide me life, betide me death,
    My love I'll gang and see ;
Altho' her friends they do me hate,
    Her love is great for me.

Of my coat I'll make a boat,
    And o' my sark a sail;
And o' my cane a gude tapmast,
    Dry land till I come till.

Then o' his coat he's made a boat,
    And o' his sark a sail ;
And o' his cane a gude tapmast,
    Dry land till he came till.

He is on to Annie's bower door,
    And tirled at the pin ;—
O sleep ye, wake ye, my love, Annie,
    Ye'll rise lat me come in.

O who is this at my bower door,
    Sae well that kens my name ?
It is your true love, sweet Willie,
    For you I've cross'd the faem.

I am deeply sworn, Willie,
　By father and by mother ;
At kirk or market where we meet,
　We dar'na own each other.

And I am deeply sworn, Willie,
　By my bauld brothers three ;
At kirk or market where we meet,
　I dar'na speak to thee.

Ye take your red fan in your hand,
　Your white fan ower your een ;
And ye may swear, and save your oath,
　Ye saw'na me come in.

Ye take me in your arms twa,
　And carry me to your bed ;
And ye may swear, and save your oath,
　Your bower I never tread.

She's ta'en her red fan in her hand,
　The white fan ower her een ;
It was to swear, and save her oath,
　She saw'na him come in.

She's ta'en him in her arms twa,
　And carried him to her bed ;
It was to swear and save her oath,
　Her bower he never tread.

They hadna kiss'd nor love clapped,
   As lovers do when they meet ;
Till up it waukens her mother,
   Out o' her drowsy sleep.

Win up, win up, my three bauld sons,
   Win up and make ye boun' ;
Your sister's lover's in her bower,
   And he's but new come in.

Then up it raise her three bauld sons,
   And girt to them their brand ;
And they are to their sister's bower
   As fast as they cou'd gang.

When they came to their sister's bower,
   They sought it up and down ;
But there was neither man nor boy,
   In her bower to be foun'.

Then out it speaks the first o' them,
   We'll gang and lat her be ;
For there is neither man nor boy
   Intill her companie.

Then out it speaks the second son,
   Our travel's a' in vain ;
But mother dear, nor father dear,
   Shall break our rest again.

Then out it speaks the third o' them,
  (An ill death mat he die !)
We'll lurk among the bent sae brown,
  That Willie we may see.

He stood behind his love's curtains,
  His goud rings show'd him light ;
And by this ye may a' weell guess,
  He was a renowned knight.

He's done him to his love's stable,
  Took out his berry brown steed ;
His love stood at her bower doer,
  Her heart was like to bleed.

O mourn ye for my coming, love ?
  Or for my short staying ?
Or mourn ye for our safe sind'ring,
  Case we never meet again ?

I mourn nae for your here coming,
  Nor for your staying lang ;
Nor mourn I for our safe sind'ring,—
  I hope we'll meet again.

I wish ye may won safe away,
  And safely frae the town,
For ken you not my brothers three
  Are 'mang the bent sae brown.

If I were on my berry-brown steed,
  And three miles frae the town,
I wouldna fear your three bauld brothers,
  Amang the bent sae brown.

He leint him ower his saddle bow,
  And kiss'd her lips sae sweet ;
The tears that fell between these twa,
  They wat his great steed's feet.

But he wasna on his berry-brown steed,
  Nor twa miles frae the town,
Till up it starts these three fierce men,
  Amang the bent sae brown.

Then up they came like three fierce men,
  Wi' mony shout and cry ;
Bide still, bide still, ye cowardly youth,
  What makes your haste away ?

For I must know before you go,
  Tell me, and make nae lie ;—
If ye've been in my sister's bower,
  My hands shall gar ye die.

Tho' I've been in your sister's bower,
  I have nae fear o' thee ;
I'll stand my ground, and fiercely fight,
  And shall gain victorie.

Now I entreat you for to stay,
   Unto us gie a wad ;
If ye our words do not obey,
   I'se gar your body bleed.

I have nae wad, says sweet Willy,
   Unless it be my brand ;
And that shall guard my fair body,
   Till I win frae your hand.

Then twa o' them stept in behind,
   All in a furious meed ;
The third o' them came hin before,
   And seiz'd his berry-brown steed.

O then he drew his trusty brand,
   That hang down by his gare ;
And he has slain these three fierce men,
   And left them sprawling there.

Then word has gane to her mother,
   In bed where she slept soun' :
That Willie had kill'd her three bauld sons,
   Amaug the bent sae brown.

Then she has cut the locks that hung
   Sae low down by her ee ;
Sae has she kiltit her green claithing
   A little aboon her knee.

And she has on to the king's court,
   As fast as gang cou'd she ;
When fair Annie got word o' that,
   Was there as soon as she.

Her mother when before the king,
   Fell low down on her knee :
Win up, win up, my dame, he said,
   What is your will wi' me ?

My wills they are not sma', my liege,
   The truth I'll tell to thee :
There is ane o' your courtly knights
   Last night hae robbed me.

And has he broke your bigly bowers,
   Or has stole your fee ?
There is nae knight into my court
   Last night has been frae me ;

Unless 'twas Willie o' Lauderdale,
   Forbid that it be he !
And by my sooth, says the auld woman,
   That very man is he.

For he has broke my bigly bowers,
   And he has stole my fee ;
And made my daughter, Ann, a whore,
   And an ill woman is she.

That was not all he did to me,
   Ere he went frae the town ;
My sons sae true he fiercely slew,
   Among the bent sae brown.

Then out it spake her daughter Ann,
   She stood by the king's knee ;
Ye lie, ye lie, my mother dear,
   Sae loud's I hear you lie.

He has not broke your bigly bowers,
   Nor has he stole your fee ;
Nor made your daughter, Ann, a whore,
   A good woman I'll be.

Altho' he slew your three bauld sons,
   He weel might be forgien ;
They were well clad in armour bright,
   Whan my love was him lane.

Well spoke, well spoke, the king replied,
   This tauking pleases me ;
For ae kiss o' your lovely mouth,
   I'll set your true love free.

She's taen the king in her arms,
   And kiss'd him cheek and chin ;
He then set her behind her love,
   And they went singing hame.

Leesome Brand.

My boy was scarcely ten years auld,
   When he went to an unco land,
Where wind never blew, nor cocks ever crew,
   Ohon ! for my son, Leesome Brand.

Awa' to that king's court he went,
   It was to serve for meat an' fee ;
Gude red gowd it was his hire,
   And lang in that king's court stay'd he.

He hadna been in that unco land,
   But only twallmonths twa or three ;
Till by the glancing o' his ee,
   He gain'd the love o' a gay ladye.

This ladye was scarce eleven years auld,
   When on her love she was right bauld ;
She was scarce up to my right knee,
   When oft in bed wi' men I'm tauld.

But when nine months were come and gane,
This ladye's face turn'd pale and wane,
To Leesome Brand she then did say,
In this place I can nae mair stay.

Ye do you to my father's stable,
Where steeds do stand baith wight and able ;
Strike ane o' them upo' the back,
The swiftest will gie his head a wap.

Ye take him out upo' the green,
And get him saddled and bridled seen ;
Get ane for you, anither for me,
And lat us ride out ower the lee.

Ye do you to my mother's coffer,
And out of it ye'll take my tocher ;
Therein are sixty thousand pounds,
Which all to me by right belongs.

He's done him to her father's stable,
Where steeds stood baith wicht and able ;
Then he strake ane upon the back,
The swiftest gae his head a wap.

He's ta'en him out upo' the green,
And got him saddled and bridled seen ;
Ane for him, and another for her,
To carry them baith wi' might and virr.

He's done him to her mother's coffer,
And there he's taen his lover's tocher ;
Wherein were sixty thousand pound,
Which all to her by right belong'd.

When they had ridden about six mile,
His true love then began to fail ;
O wae's me, said that gay ladye,
I fear my back will gang in three !

O gin I had but a gude midwife,
Here this day to save my life;
And ease me o' my misery,
O dear how happy I wou'd be !

My love, we're far frae ony town,
There is nae midwife to be foun';
But if ye'll be content wi' me,
I'll do for you what man can dee.

For no, for no, this maunna be,
Wi' a sigh, replied this gay ladye;
When I endure my grief and pain,
My companie ye maun refrain.

Ye'll take your arrow and your bow,
And ye will hunt the deer and roe;
Be sure ye touch not the white hynde,
For she is o' the woman kind.

He took sic pleasure in deer and roe,
Till he forgot his gay ladye;
Till by it came that milk-white hynde,
And then he mind on his ladye syne.

He hasted him to yon greenwood tree,
For to relieve his gay ladye;
But found his ladye lying dead,
Likeways her young son at her head.

His mother lay ower her castle wa',
   And she beheld baith dale and down ;
And she beheld young Leesome Brand,
   As he came riding to the town.

Get minstrels for to play, she said,
   And dancers to dance in my room ;
For here comes my son, Leesome Brand,
   And he comes merrilie to the town.

Seek nae minstrels to play, mother,
   Nor dancers to dance in your room ;
But tho' your son comes, Leesome Brand,
   Yet he comes sorry to the town.

O I hae lost my gowden knife,
I rather had lost my ain sweet life ;
And I hae lost a better thing,
The gilded sheath that it was in.

Are there nae gowdsmiths here in Fife,
Can make to you anither knife ?
Are there nae sheath-makers in the land,
Can make a sheath to Leesome Brand !

There are nae gowdsmiths here in Fife,
Can make me sic a gowden knife ;
Nor nae sheath-makers in the land,
Can make to me a sheath again.

There ne'er was man in Scotland born,
Ordain'd to be so much forlorn ;
I've lost my ladye I lov'd sae dear,
Likeways the son she did me bear.

Put in your hand at my bed head,
    There ye'll find a gude gray horn ;
In it three draps o' Saint Paul's ain blude,
    That hae been there sin' he was born.

Drap twa o' them o' your ladye,
    And ane upo' your little young son ;
Then as lively they will be
    As the first night ye brought them hame.

He put his hand at her bed head,
    And there he found a gude gray horn ;
Wi' three draps o' Saint Paul's ain blude,
    That had been there sin' he was born.

Then he drapp'd twa on his ladye,
    And ane o' them on his young son ;
And now they do as lively be,
    As the first day he brought them hame.

Clerk Tamas.

Clerk Tamas lov'd her, fair Annie,
    As well as Mary lov'd her son ;
But now he hates her, fair Annie,
    And hates the lands that she lives in.

Ohon, alas! said fair Annie,
  Alas! this day I fear I'll die;
But I will on to sweet Tamas,
  And see gin he will pity me.

As Tamas lay ower his shott window,
  Just as the sun was gaen down,
There he beheld her, fair Annie,
  As she came walking to the town.

O where are a' my well-wight men,
  I wat, that I pay meat and fee,
For to lat a' my hounds gang loose,
  To hunt this vile whore to the sea.

The hounds they knew the lady well,
  And nane o' them they wou'd her bite;
Save ane that is ca'd Gaudy-where,
  I wat he did the lady smite.

O wae mat worth ye, Gaudy-where,
  An ill reward this is to me,
For ae bit that I gae the lave,
  I'm very sure I've gi'en you three.

For me, alas! there's nae remeid,
  Here comes the day that I maun die;
I ken ye lov'd your master well,
  And sae, alas! for me, did I!

A captain lay ower his ship window,
    Just as the sun was gaen down ;
There he beheld her, fair Annie,
    As she was hunted frae the town.

Gin ye'll forsake father and mither,
    And sae will ye your friends and kin,
Gin ye'll forsake your lands sae broad,
    Then come and I will take you in.

Yes, I'll forsake baith father and mither,
    And sae will I my friends and kin,
Yes, I'll forsake my lands sae broad,
    And come, gin ye will take me in.

Then a' thing gaed frae fause Tamas,
    And there was naething byde him wi' ;
Then he thought lang for Arrandella,
    It was fair Annie for to see.

How do ye now, ye sweet Tamas ?
    And how gaes a' in your countrie ?
I'll do better to you than ever I've done,
    Fair Annie, gin ye'll come an' see.

O Guid forbid, said fair Annie,
    That e'er the like fa' in my hand ;
Wou'd I forsake my ain gude lord,
    And follow you, a gae-through-land ?

Yet nevertheless, now sweet Tamas,
   Ye'll drink a cup o' wine wi' me ;
And nine times in the live lang day,
   Your fair claithing shall changed be.

Fair Annie pat it till her cheek,
   Sae did she till her milk-white chin,
Sae did she till her flattering lips,
   But never a drap o' wine gaed in.

Tamas pat it till his cheek,
   Sae did he till his dimpled chin ;
He pat it till his rosy lips,
   And then the well o' wine gaed in.

These pains, said he, are ill to bide ;
   Here is the day that I maun die ;
O take this cup frae me, Annie,
   For o' the same I am weary.

And sae was I, o' you, Tamas,
   When I was hunted to the sea ;
But I'se gar bury you in state,
   Which is mair than ye'd done to me.

The Queen of Scotland.

O Troy Muir, my lily flower,
   An asking I'll ask thee ;
Will ye come to my bigley bower,
   And drink the wine wi' me !

My dame, this is too much honour
    You have conferr'd on me ;
I'm sure it's mair than I've deserv'd
    Frae sic a one as thee.

In Reekie's towers I ha'e a bower,
    And pictures round it set ;
There is a bed that is well made,
    Where you and I shall sleep.

O God forbid, this youth then said,
    That ever I drie sic blame ;
As ever to touch the queen's bodie,
    Altho' the king's frae hame.

When that he had these words spoken,
    She secretly did say ;—
Some evil I shall work this man,
    Before that it be day.

Whan a' her maids were gane to bed,
    And knights were gane frae hame ;
She call'd upon young Troy Muir,
    To put fire in her room.

An asking, asking, Troy Muir,
    An asking ye'll grant me ;
O, if it be a lawful thing,
    My dame it's granted be.

There is a stane in yon garden,
  Nae ane lifts it for me ;
But if that ye wou'd lift the same,
  A brave man I'll ca' thee.

Under yon stane there is a pit,
  Most dreary for to see ;
And in it there's as much red gowd
  As buy a dukedom to thee.

O, if I had ae sleep in bed,
  And saw the morning sun ;
As soon's I rise and see the skies,
  Your will it shall be done.

When birds did sing, and sun did rise,
  And sweetly sang the lark ;
Troy Muir to the garden went,
  To work this dreary wark.

He's ta'en the stane then by a ring,
  And lifted manfullie ;
A serpent that lang wanted meat,
  Round Troy Muir's middle did flee.

How shall I get rid o' this foul beast,
  It's by it I must die ;
I never thought the queen, my friend,
  Wou'd work this mischief to me.

But by there came a weelfair'd may,
   As Troy Muir did tauk ;
The serpent's furious rage to lay,
   Cut off her fair white pap.

As soon as she the same had done,
   Young Troy Muir was set free ;
And in ane hour the wound was heal'd
   That nae mair pain had she.

Says Troy Muir, My lily flower,
   Ye ha'e released me ;
But before I see another day,.
   My wedded wife ye'se be.

He married her on that same day,
   Brought her to his ain hame ;
A lovely son to him she bare,
   When full nine months were gane.

As heaven was pleas'd, in a short time,
   To ease her first sad pain ;
Sae was it pleas'd, when she'd a son,
   To ha'e a pap again.

The Earl of Mar's Daughter.

It was intill a pleasant time,
   Upon a simmer's day,
The noble Earl of Mar's daughter
   Went forth to sport and play.

As thus she did amuse herself,
  Below a green aik tree,
There she saw a sprightly doo
  Set on a tower sae hie.

O Cow-me-doo, my love sae true,
  If ye'll come down to me,
Ye'se ha'e a cage o' guid red gowd
  Instead o' simple tree :

I'll put gowd hingers roun' your cage,
  And siller roun' your wa' ;
I'll gar ye shine as fair a bird
  As ony o' them a'.

But she hadnae these words well spoke,
  Nor yet these words well said,
Till Cow-me-doo flew frae the tower,
  And lighted on her head.

Then she has brought this pretty bird
  Hame to her bowers and ha' ;
And made him shine as fair a bird
  As ony o' them a'.

When day was gane, and night was come,
  About the evening tide ;
This lady spied a sprightly youth
  Stand straight up by her side.

From whence came ye, young man? she said,
  That does surprise me sair;
My door was bolted right secure;
  What way ha'e ye come here?

O had your tongue, ye lady fair,
  Lat a' your folly be;
Mind ye not on your turtle doo
  Last day ye brought wi' thee?

O tell me mair, young man, she said,
  This does surprise me now;
What country ha'e ye come frae?
  What pedigree are you?

My mither lives on foreign isles,
  She has nae mair but me;
She is a queen o' wealth and state,
  And birth and high degree.

Likewise well skill'd in magic spells,
  As ye may plainly see;
And she transform'd me to yon shape,
  To charm such maids as thee.

I am a doo the live lang day,
  A sprightly youth at night;
This aye gars me appear mair fair
  In a fair maiden's sight.

And it was but this verra day
   That I came ower the sea ;
Your lovely face did me enchant,—
   I'll live and dee wi' thee.

O Cow-me-doo, my luve sae true,
   Nae mair frae me ye'se gae.
That's never my intent, my luve,
   As ye said, it shall be sae.

O Cow-me-doo, my luve sae true,
   It's time to gae to bed.
Wi' a' my heart, my dear marrow,
   It's be as ye ha'e said.

Then he has staid in bower wi' her
   For sax lang years and ane,
Till sax young sons to him she bare,
   And the seventh she's brought hame.

But aye as ever a child was born,
   He carried them away ;
And brought them to his mither's care,
   As fast as he cou'd fly.

Thus he has staid in bower wi' her
   For twenty years and three ;
There came a lord o' high renown
   To court this fair ladie.

But still his proffer she refused,
   And a' his presents too ;
Says, I'm content to live alane
   Wi' my bird, Cow-me-doo.

  Her father sware a solemn oath
    Amang the nobles all,
The morn, or ere I eat or drink,
    This bird I will gar kill.

The bird was sitting in his cage,
   And heard what they did say ;
And when he found they were dismist,
   Says, Waes me for this day.

Before that I do langer stay,
   And thus to be forlorn,
I'll gang unto my mither's bower,
   Where I was bred and born.

Then Cow-me-doo took flight and flew
   Beyond the raging sea ;
And lighted near his mither's castle
   On the tower o' gowd sae hie.

As his mither was wauking out,
   To see what she cou'd see ;
And there she saw her little son
   Set on the tower sae hie.

Get dancers here to dance, she said,
   And minstrells for to play ;
For here's my young son, Florentine,
   Come here wi' me to stay.

Get nae dancers to dance, mither,
   Nor minstrells for to play ;
For the mither o' my seven sons,
   The morn's her wedding-day.

O tell me, tell me, Florentine,
   Tell me, and tell me true ;
Tell me this day without a flaw,
   What I will do for you.

Instead of dancers to dance, mither,
   Or minstrells for to play ;
Turn four-and-twenty wall-wight men
   Like storks, in feathers gray ;

My seven sons in seven swans,
   Aboon their heads to flee ;
And I mysell, a gay gos-hawk,
   A bird o' high degree.

Then sichin' said the queen hersell,
   That thing's too high for me ;
But she applied to an auld woman,
   Who had mair skill than she.

Instead o' dancers to dance a dance,
    Or minstrells for to play ;
Four-and-twenty wall-wight men
    Turn'd birds o' feathers gray ;

Her seven sons in seven swans,
    Aboon their heads to flee ;
And he, himsell, a gay gos-hawk,
    A bird o' high degree.

This flock o' birds took flight and flew
    Beyond the raging sea ;
And landed near the Earl Mar's castle,
    Took shelter in every tree.

They were a flock o' pretty birds
    Right comely to be seen ;
The people view'd them wi' surprise
    As they danc'd on the green.

These birds ascended frae the tree,
    And lighted on the ha' ;
And at the last wi' force did flee
    Amang the nobles a'.

The storks there seized some o' the men,
    They cou'd neither fight nor flee ;
The swans they bound the bride's best man
    Below a green aik tree.

They lighted next on maidens fair,
  Then on the bride's own head;
And wi' the twinkling o' an e'e,
  The bride and them were fled.

There's ancient men at weddings been,
  For sixty years or more;
But sic a curious wedding-day
  They never saw before.

For naething cou'd the companie do,
  Nor naething cou'd they say;
But they saw a flock o' pretty birds
  That took their bride away.

When that Earl Mar, he came to know,
  Where his dochter did stay;
He sign'd a bond o' unity,
  And visits now they pay.

Death of Lord Warriston.

My mother was an ill woman,
  In fifteen years she married me;
I hadna wit to guide a man,
  Alas! ill counsell guided me.

O Warriston, O Warriston,
  I wish that ye may sink for sin;
I was but bare fifteen years auld,
  When first I enter'd your yates within.

I hadna been a month married,
  Till my gude lord went to the sea ;
I bare a bairn ere he came hame,
  And set it on the nourice knee.

But it fell ance upon a day,
  That my gude lord return'd from sea ;
Then I did dress in the best array,
  As blythe as ony bird on tree.

I took my young son in my arms,
  Likewise my nourice me forebye ;
And I went down to yon shore side,
  My gude lord's vessel I might spy.

My lord he stood upon the deck,
  I wyte he hail'd me courteouslie ;
Ye are thrice welcome, my lady gay,
  Whase aught that bairn on your knee ?

She turn'd her right and round about,
  Says, Why take ye sic dreads o' me ?
Alas ! I was too young married,
  To love another man but thee.

Now hold your tongue, my lady gay,
  Nae mair falsehoods ye'll tell to me ;
This bonny bairn is not mine,
  You've loved another while I was on sea.

In discontent, then hame she went,
    And aye the tear did blin' her e'e ;
Says, Of this wretch I'll be revenged,
    For these harsh words he's said to me.

She's counsell'd wi' her father's steward,
    What way she cou'd revenged be ;
Bad was the counsel then he gave,—
    It was to gar her gude lord dee.

The nourice took the deed in hand,
    I wat she was well paid her fee ;
She kiest the knot, and the loop she ran,
    Which soon did gar this young lord dee.

His brother lay in a room hard by,
    Alas ! that night he slept too soun' ;
But then he waken'd wi' a cry,
    I fear my brother's putten down.

O get me coal and candle light,
    And get me some gude companie ;
But before the light was brought,
    Warriston he was gart dee.

They've ta'en the lady and fause nourice,
    In prison strong they ha'e them boun' ;
The nourice she was hard o' heart,
    But the bonny lady fell in swoon.

In it came her brother dear,
   And aye a sorry man was he ;
I wou'd gie a' the lands I heir,
   O bonny Jean, to borrow thee.

O borrow me, brother, borrow me,—
   O borrow'd shall I never be ;
For I gart kill my ain gude lord,
   And life is nae pleasure to me.

In it came her mother dear,
   I wyte a sorry woman was she ;
I wou'd gie my white monie and gowd,
   O bonny Jean, to borrow thee.

Borrow me, mother, borrow me,—
   O borrow'd shall I never be ;
For I gart kill my ain gude lord,
   And life's now nae pleasure to me.

Then in it came her father dear,
   I wyte a sorry man was he ;
Says, Ohon ! alas ! my bonny Jean,
   If I had you at hame wi' me.

Seven daughters I ha'e left at hame,
   As fair women as fair can be ;
But I wou'd gi'e them ane by ane,
   O bonny Jean, to borrow thee.

O borrow me, father, borrow me,—
   O borrow'd shall I never be ;
I that is worthy o' the death,
   It is but right that I shou'd dee.

Then out it speaks the king himsell,
   And aye as he steps in the fleer ;
Says, I grant you your life, lady,
   Because you are of tender year.

A boon, a boon, my liege the king,
   The boon I ask, ye'll grant to me.
Ask on, ask on, my bonny Jean,
   Whate'er ye ask it's granted be.

Cause take me out at night, at night,
   Lat not the sun upon me shine ;
And take me to yon heading hill,
   Strike aff this dowie head o' mine.

Ye'll take me out at night, at night,
   When there are nane to gaze and see ;
And ha'e me to yon heading hill,
   And ye'll gar head me speedilie.

They've ta'en her out at nine at night,
   Loot not the sun upon her shine ;
And had her to yon heading hill,
   And headed her baith neat and fine.

Then out it speaks the king himsell,
   I wyte a sorry man was he ;
I've travell' east, I've travell'd west,
   And sail'd far beyond the sea,
But I never saw a woman's face
   I was sae sorry to see dee.

But Warriston was sair to blame,
   For slighting o' his lady so ;
He had the wyte o' his ain death,
   And bonny lady's overthrow.

Earl Crawford.

O we were seven bonny sisters,
   As fair women as fair could be,
And some got lairds, and some got lords,
   And some got knights o' high degree ;
When I was married to Earl Crawford,
   This was the fate befell to me.

When we had been married for some time,
   We walked in our garden green ;
And aye he clapp'd his young son's head,
   And aye he made sae much o' him.

I turn'd me right and round about,
   And aye the blythe blink in my e'e ;
Ye think as much o' your young son
   As ye do o' my fair body.

What need ye clap your young son's head,
   What need ye make so much o' him?
What need ye clap your young son's head?
   I'm sure ye gotna him your lane.

O if I gotna him my lane,
   Show here the man that helped me;
And for these words your ain mouth spoke,
   Heir o' my land he ne'er shall be.

He call'd upon his stable groom,
   To come to him right speedilie;
·Gae saddle a steed to Lady Crawford,
   Be sure ye do it hastilie.

His bridle gilt wi' gude red gowd,
   That it may glitter in her e'e;
And send her on to bonny Stobha',
   All her relations for to see.

Her mother lay o'er the castle wa',
   And she beheld baith dale and down;
And she beheld her, Lady Crawford,
   As she came riding to the town.

Come here, come here, my husband dear,
   This day ye see not what I see;
For here there comes her, Lady Crawford,
   Riding alane upon the lee.

When she came to her father's yates,
　　She tirled gently at the pin;
If ye sleep, awake, my mother dear,
　　Ye'll rise lat Lady Crawford in.

What news, what news, ye Lady Crawford,
　　That ye come here so hastilie?
Bad news, bad news, my mother dear,
　　For my gude lord's forsaken me.

O wae's me for you, Lady Crawford,
　　This is a dowie tale to me;
Alas! you were too young married,
　　To thole sic cross and misery.

O had your tongue, my mother dear,
　　And ye'll lat a' your folly be;
It was a word my merry mouth spake,
　　That sinder'd my gude lord and me.

Out it spake her brither then,
　　Aye as he stept ben the floor;
My sister Lillie was but eighteen years
　　When Earl Crawford ca'ed her a whore.

But had your tongue, my sister dear,
　　And ye'll lat a' your mourning bee;
I'll wed you to as fine a knight,
　　That is nine times as rich as hee.

O had your tongue, my brither dear,
   And ye'll lat a' your folly bee ;
I'd rather yae kiss o' Crawford's mouth
   Than a' his gowd and white monie.

But saddle to me my riding steed,
   And see him saddled speedilie ;
And I will on to Earl Crawford's,
   And see if he will pity me.

Earl Crawford lay o'er castle wa',
   And he beheld baith dale and down ;
And he beheld her, Lady Crawford,
   As she came riding to the town.

He called ane o' his livery men
   To come to him right speedilie ;
Gae shut my yates, gae steek my doors,
   Keep Lady Crawford out frae me.

When she came to Earl Crawford's yates,
   She tirled gently at the pin ;
O sleep ye, wake ye, Earl Crawford,
   Ye'll open, lat Lady Crawford in.

Come down, come down, O Earl Crawford,
   And speak some comfort unto me ;
And if ye winna come yoursell,
   Ye'll send your gentleman to me.

Indeed, I winna come mysell,
    Nor send my gentleman to thee;
For I tauld you when we did part
    Nae mair my spouse ye'd ever bee.

She laid her mouth then to the yates,
    And aye the tears drapt frae her e'e;
Says, Fare-ye-well, Earl Crawford's yates,
    You, again, I'll nae mair see.

Earl Crawford call'd on his stable groom
    To come to him right speedilie;
And sae did he his waiting man,
    That did attend his fair bodie.

Ye will gae saddle for me my steed,
    And see and saddle him speedilie;
And I'll gang to the Lady Crawford,
    And see if she will pity me.

Lady Crawford lay o'er castle wa'.
    And she beheld baith dale and down;
And she beheld him, Earl Crawford,
    As he came riding to the town.

Then she has call'd ane o' her maids
    To come to her right speedilie;
Gae shut my yates, gae steek my doors,
    Keep Earl Crawford out frae me.

When he came to Lady Crawford's yates,
　　He tirled gently at the pin ;
Sleep ye, wake ye, Lady Crawford,
　　Ye'll rise and lat Earl Crawford in.

Come down, come down, O Lady Crawford,
　　Come down, come down, and speak wi' me ;
And gin ye winna come yoursell,
　　Ye'll send your waiting-maid to me.

Indeed I winna come mysell,
　　Nor send my waiting-maid to thee ;
Sae take your ain words hame again
　　At Crawford castle ye tauld me.

O mother, dear, gae make my bed,
　　And ye will make it saft and soun',
And turn my face unto the west,
　　That I nae mair may see the sun.

Her mother she did make her bed,
　　And she did make it saft and soun' ;
True were the words fair Lillie spake,
　　Her lovely eyes ne'er saw the sun.

The Earl Crawford mounted his steed,
　　Wi' sorrows great he did ride hame ;
But ere the morning sun appear'd,
　　This fine lord was dead and gane.

Then on a'e night this couple died,
  And baith were buried in a'e tomb ;
Let this a warning be to all,
  Their pride may not bring them low down.

Rose the Red and White Lillie.

Now word is gane thro' a' the land,
  Gude seal that it sae spread !
To Rose the Red and White Lillie,
  Their mither dear was dead.

Their father's married a bauld woman,
  And brought her ower the sea ;
Twa sprightly youths, her ain young sons,
  Intill her companie.

They fix'd their eyes on those ladies,
  On shipboard as they stood,
And sware, if ever they wan to land,
  These ladies they wou'd wed.

But there was nae a quarter past,
  A quarter past but three,
Till these young luvers a' were fond
  O' others companie.

The knights they harped i' their bower,
　The ladies sewed and sang ;
There was mair mirth in that chamer
　Than a' their father's lan'.

Then out it spak their step-mither,
　At the stair-foot stood she ;
I'm plagued wi' your troublesome noise,
　What makes your melodie ?

O Rose the Red, ye sing too loud,
　While Lillie your voice is strang ;
But gin I live and brook my life,
　I'se gar you change your sang.

We maunna change our loud, loud song,
　For nae Duke's son ye'll bear ;
We winna change our loud, loud song,
　But aye we'll sing the mair.

We never sung the sang, mither,
　But we'll sing ower again ;
We'll take our harps into our hands,
　And we'll harp, and we'll sing.

She's call'd upon her twa young sons,
　Says, Boun' ye for the sea ;
Let Rose the Red, and White Lillie,
　Stay in their bower wi' me.

O God forbid, said her eldest son,
  Nor lat it ever be,
Unless ye were as kind to our luves
  As gin we were them wi'.

Yet never the less, my pretty sons,
  Ye'll boun' you for the faem;
Let Rose the Red, and White Lillie,
  Stay in their bowers at hame.

O when wi' you we came alang,
  We felt the stormy sea;
And where we go, ye ne'er shall know,
  Nor shall be known by thee.

Then wi' her harsh and boisterous word,
  She forc'd these lads away;
While Rose the Red, and White Lillie
  Still in their bowers did stay.

But there was not a quarter past,
  A quarter past but ane;
Till Rose the Red in rags she gaed,
  White Lillie's claithing grew thin.

Wi' bitter usage every day,
  The ladies they thought lang;
Ohon, alas! said Rose the Red,
  She's gar'd us change our sang.

But we will change our own fu' names,
　And we'll gang frae the town ;
Frae Rose the Red and White Lillie,
　To Nicholas and Roger Brown.

And we will cut our green claithing
　A little aboon our knee ;
And we will on to gude greenwood,
　Twa bauld bowmen to be.

Ohon, alas ! said White Lillie,
　My fingers are but sma' ;
And tho' my hands wou'd wield the bow,
　They winna yield at a'.

O had your tongue now, White Lillie,
　And lat these fears a' be ;
There's naething that ye're awkward in,
　But I will learn thee.

Then they are on to gude greenwood
　As fast as gang cou'd they ;
O then they spied him, Robin Hood,
　Below a green aik tree.

Gude day, gude day, kind sir, they said,
　God make you safe and free.
Gude day, gude day, said Robin Hood,
　What is your wills wi' me ?

Lo here we are, twa banish'd knights,
   Come frae our native hame;
We're come to crave o' thee service,
   Our king will gie us nane.

If ye be twa young banish'd knights,
   Tell me frae what countrie;
Frae Anster town into Fifeshire,
   Ye know it as well as we.

If a' be true that ye ha'e said,
   And tauld just now to me;
Ye're welcome, welcome, every one,
   Your master I will be.

Now ye shall eat as I do eat,
   And lye as I do lye;
Ye salna wear nae waur claithing
   Nor my young men and I.

Then they went to a ruinous house,
   And there they enter'd in;
And Nicholas fed wi' Robin Hood,
   And Roger wi' little John.

But it fell ance upon a day,
   They were at the putting-stane;
Whan Rose the Red she view'd them a',
   As they stood on the green.

She hit the stane then wi' her foot,
   And kep'd it wi' her knee ;
And spaces three aboon them a',
   I wyte she gar'd it flee.

She set her back then to a tree,
   And ga'e a loud Ohon !
A lad spak in the companie,
   I hear a woman's moan.

How know you that, young man, she said,
   How know you that o' me ?
Did e'er ye see me in that place,
   A'e foot my ground to flee ?

Or know ye by my cherry cheeks,
   Or by my yellow hair ;
Or by the paps on my breast bane,
   Ye never saw them bare.

I know not by your cherry cheeks,
   Nor by your yellow hair ;
But I know by your milk-white chin,
   On it there grows nae hair.

I never saw you in that cause
   A'e foot your ground to flee ;
I've seen you stan' wi' sword in han'
   'Mang men's blood to the knee.

But if I come your bower within,
   By night or yet by day;
I shall know, before I go,
   If ye be man or may.

O if you come my bower within,
   By night, or yet by day,
As soon's I draw my trusty brand,
   Nae lang ye'll wi' me stay.

But he is haunted to her bower,
   Her bigly bower o' stane,
Till he has got her big wi' bairn,
   And near six months she's gane.

Whan three mair months were come and gane,
   They gae'd to hunt the hynde;
She wont to be the foremost ane,
   But now stay'd far behynd.

Her luver looks her in the face,
   And thus to her said he;
I think your cheeks are pale and wan,
   Pray, what gaes warst wi' thee?

O want ye roses to your breast,
   Or ribbons to your sheen?
Or want ye as muckle o' dear bought luve
   As your heart can conteen?

I want nae roses to my breast,
  Nae ribbons to my sheen ;
Nor want I as muckle dear bought luve
  As my heart can conteen.

I'd rather ha'e a fire behynd,
  Anither me before ;
A gude midwife at my right side,
  Till my young babe be bore.

I'll kindle a fire wi' a flint stane,
  Bring wine in a horn green ;
I'll be midwife at your right side,
  Till your young babe be born.

That was ne'er my mither's custom,
  Forbid that it be mine !
A knight stan' by a lady bright,
  When she drees a' her pine.

There is a knight in gude greenwood,
  If that he kent o' me ;
Thro' stock and stane, and the hawthorn,
  Sae soon's he wou'd come me tee.

If there be a knight in gude greenwood
  Ye like better than me ;
If ance he come your bower within,
  Ane o' us twa shall dee.

She set a horn to her mouth,
   And she blew loud and shrill;
Thro' stock and stane, and the hawthorn,
   Brave Roger came her till.

Wha's here sae bauld, the youth replied,
   Thus to encroach on me?
O here am I, the knight replied,
   Ha'e as much right as thee.

Then they fought up the gude greenwood,
   Sae did they down the plain;
They niddart ither wi' lang braid swords,
   Till they were bleedy men.

Then out it spak the sick woman,
   Sat under the greenwood tree;
O had your han', young man, she said,
   She's a woman as well as me.

Then out it speaks anither youth,
   Amang the companie;
Gin I had kent what I ken now,
   'Tis for her I wou'd dee.

O wae mat worth you, Rose the Red,
   An ill death mat ye dee!
Altho' ye tauld upo' yoursell,
   Ye might ha'e heal'd on me.

O for her sake I was content
  For to gae ower the sea ;
For her I left my mither's ha',
  Tho' she proves fause to me.

But when these luvers were made known,
  They sung right joyfullie ;
Nae blyther was the nightingale,
  Nor bird that sat on tree.

Now they ha'e married these ladies,
  Brought them to bower and ha',
And now a happy life they lead,
  I wish sae may we a'.

Burd Isbel and Sir Patrick.

Take warning a' ye young women,
  Of low station or hie ;
Lay never your love upon a man
  Above your ain degree.

Thus I speak by Burd Isbel,
  She was a maid sae fair ;
She laid her love on Sir Patrick,
  She'll rue it for evermair.

And likewise a' ye sprightly youths
  Of low station or hie ;
Lay never your love upon a maid
  Below your ain degree.

And thus I speak by Sir Patrick,
  Who was a knight sae rare ;
He's laid his love on Burd Isbel,
  He'll rue it for evermair.

Burd Isbel was but ten years auld,
  To service she has gane ;
And Burd Isbel was but fifteen
  Whan her young son came hame.

It fell ance upon a day,
  Strong travelling took she ;
None there was her bower within,
  But Sir Patrick and she.

This is a wark now, Sir Patrick,
  That we twa ne'er will end ;
Ye'll do you to the outer court,
  And call some women in.

He's done him to the outer court,
  And stately there did stand ;
Eleven ladies he's call'd in
  Wi' a'e shake o' his hand.

Be favourable to Burd Isbel,
   Deal favourable if ye may ;
Her kirking and her fair wedding,
   Shall baith stand on ae day,

Deal favourable to Burd Isbel,
   Whom I love as my life ;
Ere this day month be come and gane,
   She's be my wedded wife.

Then he is on to his father,
   Fell low down on his knee ;
Says, Will I marry Burd Isbel ?
   She's born a son to me.

O marry, marry Burd Isbel,
   Or use her as ye like ;
Ye'll gar her wear the silks sae red,
   And sae may ye the white.
O wou'd ye marry Burd Isbel,
   Make her your heart's delight ?

You want not lands, nor rents, Patrick,
   You know your fortune's free ;
But ere you'd marry Burd Isbel,
   I'd rather bury thee.

Ye'll build a bower for Burd Isbel,
   And set it round wi' sand ;
Make as much mirth in Isbel's bower
   As ony in a' the land.

Then he is to his mother gane,
   Fell low down on his knee ;
O shall I marry Burd Isbel ?
   She's born a son to me.

O marry, marry Burd Isbel,
   Or use her as ye like ;
Ye'll gar her wear the silks sae red,
   And sae may ye the white ;
O would ye marry Burd Isbel,
   Make her wi' me alike ?

You want not lands and rents, Patrick,
   You know your fortune's free ;
But ere you marry Burd Isbel,
   I'd rather bury thee.

Ye'll build a bower to Burd Isbel,
   And set it round wi' glass ;
Make as much mirth in Isbel's bower
   As ony in a' the place.

He's done him down thro' ha', thro' ha',
   Sae has he in thro' bower ;
The tears ran frae his twa grey eyes,
   And loot them fast down pour.

My father and my mother baith
   To age are coming on ;
When they are dead and buried baith
   Burd Isbel I'll bring home.

The words that pass'd atween these twa,
  Ought never to be spoken ;
The vows that pass'd atween these twa
  Ought never to be broken.

Says he, If I another court,
  Or wed another wife,
May eleven devils me attend
  At the end-day o' my life.

But his father he soon did die,
  His mother nae lang behind ;
But Sir Patrick of Burd Isbel
  He now had little mind.

It fell ance upon a day,
  As she went out to walk ;
And there she saw him, Sir Patrick,
  Going wi' his hound and hawk.

Stay still, stay still, now Sir Patrick,
  O stay a little wee,
And think upon the fair promise
  Last year ye made to me.

Now your father's dead, kind sir,
  And your mother the same ;
Yet nevertheless, now Sir Patrick,
  Ye're nae bringing me hame.

If the morn be a pleasant day,
　　I mean to sail the sea ;
To spend my time in fair England,
　　All for a month, or three.

He hadna been in fair England
　　A month but barely ane,
Till he forgot her, Burd Isbel,
　　The mother of his son.

Some time he spent in fair England,
　　And when return'd again,
He laid his love on a Duke's daughter,
　　And he has brought her hame.

Now he's forgot his first true love
　　He ance lov'd ower them a' ;
But now the devil did begin
　　To work between them twa.

When Sir Patrick he was wed,
　　And all set down to dine,
Upon his first love, Burd Isbel,
　　A thought ran in his mind.

He call'd upon his gude grand aunt,
　　To come right speedilie ;
Says, Ye'll gae on to Burd Isbel,
　　Bring my young son to me.

She's ta'en her mantle her about,
  Wi' gowd gloves on her hand ;
And she is on to Burd Isbel,
  As fast as she cou'd gang.

She hail'd her high, she hail'd her low,
  With stile in great degree ;
O busk, O busk your little young son,
  For he maun gang wi' me.

I wou'd fain see the one, she said,
  O' low station or hie,
Wou'd take the bairn frae my foot,
  For him I bowed my knee.

I wou'd fain see the one, she said,
  O' low station or mean,
Wou'd take the bairn frae my foot
  Whom I own to be mine.

Then she has done her hame again,
  As fast as gang cou'd she,
Present, said he, my little young son,
  For him I wish to see.

Burd Isbel's a bauld woman, she said,
  As e'er I yet spake wi',
But sighing, said him, Sir Patrick,
  She ne'er was bauld to me.

But he's dress'd in his best array,
    His gowd rod in his hand ;
And he is to Burd Isbel's bower,
    As fast as he cou'd gang.

O how is this, Burd Isbel, he said,
    So ill ye've used me ?
What gart you anger my gude grand aunt,
    That I did send to thee ?

If I ha'e anger'd your gude grand aunt,
    O then sae lat it be ;
I said naething to your gude grand aunt
    But what I'll say to thee.

I wou'd fain see the one, I said,
    O' low station or hie,
Wha wou'd take this bairn frae my foot,
    For him I bowed the knee.

I wou'd fain see the one, I said,
    O' low station or mean,
Wou'd take this bairn frae my foot.
    Whom I own to be mine.

O if I had some counsellers here,
    And clerks to seal the band,
I wou'd infeft your son, this day,
    In third part o' my land.

I ha'e two couzins, Scottish clerks.
  Wi' bills into their hand,
An' ye'll infeft my son, this day,
  In third part o' your land.

Then he call'd in her Scottish clerks,
  Wi' bills into their hand ;
And he's infeft his son that day
  The third part o' his land.

To ane o' these young clerks she spoke,
  Clerk John it was his name ;
Says, Of my son I gi'e you charge
  Till I return again.

Ye'll take here my son, clerk John,
  Learn him to dance and sing ;
And I will to some unco land,
  Drive love out of my mind.

And ye'll take here my son, clerk John,
  Learn him to hunt the roe ;
And I will to some unco land,—
  Now lat Sir Patrick go.

But I'll cause this knight at church-door stand,
  For a' his noble train ;
For selling o' his precious soul,
  Dare never come farther ben.

Charlie M'Pherson.

Charlie M'Pherson,
That brisk Highland laddie :
At Valentine even,
He came to Kinadie :

To court her, Burd Helen,
Baith waking and sleeping ;
Joy be wi' them
That has her a-keeping.

Auldtown and Muirtown,
Likewise Billy Beg ;
All gaed wi' Charlie,
For to be his guide.

Jamie M'Robbie,
Likewise Wattie Nairn,
All ga'ed wi' Charlie
For to be his warran'.

When they came to Kinadie,
They knock'd at the door ;
When nae ane wou'd answer,
They ga'ed a loud roar.

Ye'll open the door, mistress,
And lat us come in :
For tidings we've brought
Frae your appearant guid son.

For to defend them,
She was not able ;
They bang'd up the stair,
Sat down at the table.

Ye'll eat and drink, gentlemen,
And eat at your leisure ;
Nae thing's disturb you,
Take what's your pleasure.

O madam, said he,
I'm come for your daughter ;
Lang ha'e I come to Kinadie,
And there sought her.

Now she's gae wi' me
For mony a mile,
Before that I return
Unto the West Isle.

My daughter's not at home,
She is gone abroad ;
Ye darena now steal her.
Her tocher is guid.

My daughter's in Whitehouse,
Wi' Mistress Dalgairn ;
Joy be wi' them,
That waits on my bairn !

The swords an the targe,
That hang about Charlie ;
They had sic a glitter,
And set him sae rarelie ;

They had sic a glitter,
And kiest sic a glamour ;
They showed mair light,
Than they had in the chamour.

To Whitehouse he went ;
And when he came there,
Right sair was his heart.
When he went up the stair ;

Burd Helen was sitting
By Thomas' bed-side ;
And all in the house
Were addressing her, Bride.

O farewell now, Helen,
I'll bid you adieu ;
Is this a' the comfort
I'm getting frae you ?

It was never my intention
Ye shou'd be the waur ;
My heavy heart light on
Whitehouse o' Cromar !

For you I ha'e travelled
Full mony lang mile ;
Awa' to Kinadie,
Far frae the West Isle.

But now ye are married,
And I am the waur ;
My heavy heart light on
Whitehouse o' Cromar.

Charles Graeme.

Cauld, cauld blaws the winter night,
   Sair beats the heavy rain ;
Young Charles Graeme's the lad I love,
   In greenwood he lies slain.

But I will do for Charles Graeme
   What other maidens may ;
I'll sit and harp upon his grave
   A twelvemonth and a day.

She harped a' the live lang night,
   The saut tears she did weep ;
Till at the hour o' one o'clock
   His ghost began to peep.

Pale and deadly was his cheek,
  And pale, pale was his chin ;
And how and hollow were his e'en,
  No light appear'd therein.

Why sit ye here, ye maiden fair,
  To mourn sae sair for me ?
I am sae sick, and very love sick,
  Aye foot I cannot jee.

Sae well's I loved young Charles Graeme,
  I kent he loved me ;
My very heart's now like to break
  For his sweet companie.

Will ye hae an apple, lady,
  And I will sheave it sma' ?
I am sae sick, and very love sick,
  I cannot eat at a'.

Will ye hae the wine, lady,
  And I will drain it sma' ?
I am sae sick, and very love sick,
  I cannot drink at a'.

See ye not my father's castle,
  Well covered ower wi 'tin ?
There's nane has sic an anxious wish
  As I hae to be in.

O hame, fair maid, ye'se quickly won,
  But this request grant me,
When ye are safe in downbed laid,
  That I may sleep wi' thee.

If hame again, sir, I could win,
  I'll this request grant thee ;
When I am safe in downbed laid,
  This night ye'se sleep wi' me.

Then he pou'd up a birken bow,
  Pat it in her right han' ;
And they are to yon castle fair
  As fast as they cou'd gang.

When they came to yon castle fair,
  It was piled round about ;
She slipped in and bolted the yetts,
  Says, Ghaists may stand thereout.

Then he vanish'd frae her sight,
  In the twinkling o' an e'e ;
Says, Let never ane a woman trust
  Sae much as I've done thee.

The Courteous Knight.

There was a knight, in a summer's night,
  Appear'd in a lady's hall,
As she was walking up and down,
  Looking o'er her castle wall.

God make you safe and free, fair maid,
   God make you safe and free !
O sae fa' you, ye courteous knight,
   What are your wills wi' me ?

My wills wi' you are not sma', lady,
   My wills wi' you nae sma' ;
And since there's nane your bower within,
   Ye'se ha'e my secrets a'.

For here am I a courtier,
   A courtier come to thee ;
And if ye winna grant your love,
   All for your sake I'll dee.

If that ye dee for me, sir knight,
   Few for you will make meen ;
For mony gude lord's done the same,
   Their graves are growing green.

O winna ye pity me, fair maid,
   O winna ye pity me ?
O winna ye pity a courteous knight,
   Whose love is laid on thee ?

Ye say ye are a courteous knight,
   But I think ye are nane;
I think ye're but a millar bred,
   By the colour o' your claithing.

You seem to be some false young man,
　You wear your hat sae wide ;
You seem to be some false young man,
　You wear your boots sae side.

Indeed I am a courteous knight,
　And of great pedigree ;
Nae knight did mair for a lady bright
　Than I will do for thee.

O, I'll put smiths in your smithy,
　To shoe for you a steed ;
And I'll put tailors in your bower,
　To make for you a weed.

I will put cooks in your kitchen,
　And butlers in your ha' ;
And on the tap o' your father's castle,
　I big gude corn and saw.

If ye be a courteous knight,
　As I trust not ye be ;
Ye'll answer some o' the sma' questions
　That I will ask at thee.

What is the fairest flower, tell me,
　That grows in mire or dale ?
Likewise, which is the sweetest bird
　Sings next the nightingale ?

Or what's the finest thing, she says,
   That king or queen can wile ?

The primrose is the fairest flower,
   That grows in mire or dale ;
The mavis is the sweetest bird
   Next to the nightingale ;
And yellow gowd's the finest thing
   That king or queen can wale.

Ye ha'e asked many questions, lady,
   I've you as many told ;
But, how many pennies round
   Make a hundred pounds in gold ?

How many of the small fishes
   Do swim the salt seas round ?
Or, what's the seemliest sight you'll see
   Into a May morning ?

Berry-brown ale and a birken speal,
   And wine in a horn green ;
A milk-white lace in a fair maid's dress,
   Looks gay in a May morning.

Mony's the questions, I've ask'd at thee,
   And ye've answer'd them a' ;
Ye are mine, and I am thine,
   Amo' the sheets sae sma'.

You may be my match, kind sir,
　You may be my match and more ;
There ne'er was ane came sic a length,
　Wi' my father's heir before.

My father's lord o' nine castles,
　My mother she's lady ower three,
And there is nane to heir them all,
　No never a ane but me ;
Unless it be Willie, my ae brother,
　But he's far ayont the sea.

If your father's laird o' nine castles,
　Your mother lady ower three ;
I am Willie your ae brother,
　Was far beyond the sea.

If ye be Willie, my ae brother,
　As I doubt sair ye be ;
But if its true ye tell me now,
　This night I'll gang wi' thee.

Ye've ower ill-washen feet, Janet,
　And ower ill-washen hands,
And ower coarse robes on your body,
　Alang wi' me to gang.

The worms they are my bed-fellows,
　And the cauld clay my sheet ;
And the higher that the wind does blaw,
　The sounder I do sleep.

My body's buried in Dumfermline,
　　And far beyond the sea ;
But day nor night, nae rest cou'd get,
　　All for the pride o' thee.

Leave aff your pride, jelly Janet, he says,
　　Use it not ony mair ;
Or when ye come where I hae been,
　　You will repent it sair.

Cast aff, cast aff, sister, he says,
　　The gowd lace frae your crown ;
For if ye gang where I hae been,
　　Ye'll wear it laigher down.

When ye're in the gude church set,
　　The gowd pins in your hair ;
Ye take mair delight in your feckless dress
　　Than ye do in your morning prayer.

And when ye walk in the church-yard,
　　And in your dress are seen,
There is nae lady that sees your face
　　But wishes your grave were green.

You're straight and tall, handsome withall,
　　But your pride owergoes your wit ;
But if ye do not your ways refrain,
　　In Pirie's chair ye'll sit.

In Pirie's chair you'll sit, I say,
  The lowest seat o' hell;
If ye do not amend your ways,
  It's there that ye must dwell.

Wi' that he vanish'd frae her sight,
  Wi' the twinkling o' an eye;
Naething mair the lady saw,
  But the gloomy clouds and sky.

Sweet Willie and Fair Maisry.

Hey love Willie, and how love Willie,
  And Willie my love shall be;
They're thinking to sinder our lang love, Willie,
  It's mair than man can dee.

Ye'll mount me quickly on a steed,
  A milk-white steed or gray;
And carry me on to gude greenwood
  Before that it be day.

He mounted her upon a steed,
  He chose a steed o' gray;
He had her on to gude greenwood
  Before that it was day.

O will ye gang to the cards, Meggie ?
   Or will ye gang wi' me ?
Or will ye ha'e a bower woman,
   To stay ere it be day ?

I winna gang to the cards, she said,
   Nor will I gae wi' thee,
Nor will I hae a bower woman,
   To spoil my modestie.

Ye'll gie me a lady at my back,
   An' a lady me beforn ;
An' a midwife at my twa sides
   Till your young son be born.

Ye'll do me up, and further up,
   To the top o' yon greenwood tree ;
For every pain myself shall ha'e,
   The same pain ye maun drie.

The first pain that did strike sweet Willie,
   It was into the side ;
Then sighing sair, said sweet Willie,
   These pains are ill to bide.

The nextan pain that strake sweet Willie,
   It was into the back ;
Then sighing sair, said sweet Willie,
   These pains are women's wreck.

The nextan pain that strake sweet Willie,
  It was into the head ;
Then sighing sair, said sweet Willie,
  I fear my lady's dead.

Then he's gane on, and further on,
  At the foot o' yon greenwood tree ;
There he got his lady lighter,
  Wi' his young son on her knee.

Then he's ta'en up his little young son,
  And kiss'd him cheek and chin ;
And he is on to his mother,
  As fast as he could gang.

Ye will take in my son, mother,
  Gi'e him to nurses nine ;
Three to wauk, and three to sleep,
  And three to gang between.

Then he has left his mother's house,
  And frae her he has gane ;
And he is back to his lady,
  And safely brought her hame.

Then in it came her father dear,
  Was belted in a brand ;
It's nae time for brides to lye in bed,
  When the bridegroom's sends' in town.

There are four-and-twenty noble lords
  A' lighted on the green ;
The fairest knight amang them a',
  He must be your bridegroom.

O wha will shoe my foot, my foot ?
  And wha will glove my hand ?
And wha will prin my sma' middle,
  Wi' the short prin and the lang ?

Now out it speaks him, sweet Willie,
  Who knew her troubles best ;
It is my duty for to serve,
  As I'm come here as guest.

Now I will shoe your foot, Maisry,
  And I will glove your hand,
And I will prin your sma' middle,
  Wi' the sma' prin and the lang.

Wha will saddle my steed, she says,
  And gar my bridle ring ;
And wha will ha'e me to gude church-door,
  This day I'm ill abound ?

I will saddle your steed, Maisry,
  And gar your bridle ring ;
And I'll hae you to gude church-door,
  And safely set you down.

O healy, healy take me up,
   And healy set me down ;
And set my back until a wa',
   My foot to yird-fast stane.

He healy took her frae her horse,
   And healy set her down ;
And set her back until a wa',
   Her foot to yird-fast stane.

When they had eaten and well drunken,
   And a' had thorn'd fine ;
The bride's father he took the cup,
   For to serve out the wine.

Out it speaks the bridegroom's brother,
   An ill death mat he die !
I fear our bride she's born a bairn,
   Or else has it a dee.

She's ta'en out a Bible braid,
   And deeply has she sworn ;
If I ha'e born a bairn, she says,
   Sin' yesterday at morn ;

Or if I've born a bairn, she says,
   Sin' yesterday at noon ;
There's nae a lady amang you a'
   That wou'd been here sae soon.

Then out it spake the bridegroom's man,
   Mischance come ower his heel!
Win up, win up, now bride, he says,
   And dance a shamefu' reel.*

Then out it speaks the bride hersell,
   And a sorry heart had she;
Is there nae ane amang you a'
   Will dance this dance for me?

Then out it speaks him, sweet Willie,
   And he spake aye thro' pride;
O draw my boots for me, bridegroom,
   Or I dance for your bride.

Then out it spake the bride hersell,
   O na, this maunna be;
For I will dance this dance mysell,
   Tho' my back shou'd gang in three.

She hadna well gane thro' the reel,
   Nor yet well on the green,
Till she fell down at Willie's feet
   As cauld as ony stane.

He's ta'en her in his arms twa,
   And ha'ed her up the stair;
Then up it came her jolly bridegroom,
   Says, What's your business there?

* The first reel that is danced with the bride, her maiden, and
two young men, and is called the Shame Spring, or Reel, as the
bride chooses the tune that is to be played.

Then Willie lifted up his foot,
    And dang him down the stair ;
And brake three ribs o' the bridegroom's side,
    And a word he spake nae mair.

Nae meen was made for that lady,
    When she was lying dead ;
But a' was for him, sweet Willie,
    On the fields, for he ran mad.

Young Prince James.

There stands a stane in wan water,
    It's lang ere it grew green ;
Lady Maisry sits in her bower door,
    Sowing at her silken seam.

Word's gane to her mother's kitchen,
    And to her father's ha' ;
That Lady Maisry is big wi' bairn,
    And her true love's far awa'.

When her brother got word of this,
    Then fiercely looked he ;
Betide me life, betide me death,
    At Maisry's bower I'se be.

Gae saddle to me the black, the black,
    Gae saddle to me the brown ;
Gae saddle to me the swiftest steed,
    To ha'e me to the town.

When he came to Maisry's bower,
    He turn'd him round about ;
And at a little shott window,
    He saw her peeping out.

Gude morrow, gude morrow, Lady Maisry,
    God make you safe and free !
Gude morrow, gude morrow, my brother dear,
    What are your wills wi' me ?

What's come o' a' your green claithing
    Was ance for you too side ?
And what's become o' your lang stays
    Was ance for you too wide ?

O he that made my claithing short,
    I hope he'll make them side ;
And he that made my stays narrow,
    I hope he'll make them wide.

O is it to a lord o' might,
    Or baron o' high degree ?
Or is it to any o' your father's boys
    Rides in the chase him wi' ?

It's no to any Scottish lord,
  Nor baron o' high degree ;
But English James, that little prince,
  That has beguiled me.

O was there not a Scots baron
  That could ha'e fitted thee,
That thus you've lov'd an Englishman,
  And has affronted me ?

She turn'd her right and round about,
  The tear blinded her e'e ;
What is the wrang I've done, brother,
  Ye look sae fierce at me ?

Will ye forsake that English blude,
  When your young babe is born ?
I'll nae do that, my brother dear,
  Tho' I shou'd be forlorn.

I'se cause a man put up the fire,
  Anither ca' in the stake ;
And on the head o' yon high hill
  I'll burn you for his sake.

O where are all my wall-wight men,
  That I pay meat and fee ?
For to hew down baith thistle and thorn
  To burn that lady wi'.

Then he has ta'en her, Lady Maisry,
   And fast he has her bound ;
And he caus'd the fiercest o' his men
   Drag her frae town to town.

Then he has caus'd ane of his men
   Hew down baith thistle and thorn ;
She carried the peats in her petticoat lap,
   Her ainsell for to burn.

Then ane pat up this big bauld fire,
   Anither ca'd in the stake ;
It was to burn her, Lady Maisry,
   All for her true love's sake.

But it fell ance upon a day,
   Prince James he thought full lang ;
He minded on the lady gay
   He left in fair Scotland.

O where will I get a little wee boy
   Will win gowd to his fee ?
That will rin on to Adam's high tower,
   Bring tidings back to me ?

O here am I, a little wee boy,
   Will win gowd to my fee ;
That will rin on to Adam's high tower,
   Bring tidings back to thee.

Then he is on to Adam's high tower
   As fast as gang cou'd he ;
And he but only wan in time,
   The fatal sight to see.

He sat his bent bow to his breast,
   And ran right speedilie ;
And he is back to his master,
   As fast as gang cou'd he.

What news, what news, my little wee boy ?
   What news ha'e ye to me ?
Bad news, bad news, my master dear,
   Bad news, as ye will see.

Are ony o' my biggins brunt, my boy ?
   Or ony o' my towers won ?
Or is my lady lighter yet
   O' dear daughter or son ?

There's nane o' your biggins brunt, master,
   Nor nane o' your towers won,
Nor is your lady lighter yet,
   O' dear daughter nor son.

There's an has been a big bauld fire,
   Anither ca'd in the stake ;
And on the head o' yon high hill,
   They're to burn her for your sake.

Gae saddle to me the black, the black,
  Gae saddle to me the brown ;
Gae saddle to me the swiftest steed,
  To ha'e me to the town.

Ere he was three miles near the town,
  She heard his horse-foot patt ;
Mend up the fire, my fause brother,
  It scarce comes to my pap.

Ere he was twa miles near the town,
  She heard his bridle ring ;
Mend up the fire, my fause brother,
  It scarce comes to my chin.

But look about, my fause brother,
  Ye see not what I see ;
I see them coming here, or lang
  Will mend the fire for thee.

Then up it comes him, little Prince James,
  And fiercely looked he ;
I'se make my love's words very true
  She said concerning me.

O wha has been sae bauld, he said,
  As put this bonfire on ?
And wha has been sae bauld, he said,
  As put that lady in ?

Then out it spake her brother then,
   He spoke right furiouslie ;
Says, I'm the man that put her in,
   Wha dare hinder me ?

If my hands had been loose, she said,
   As they are fastly bound ;
I wou'd ha'e looted me to the ground,
   Gi'en you up your bonny young son.

I will burn for my love's sake,
   Her father and her mother ;
And I will burn for my love's sake,
   Her sister and her brother.

And I will burn for my love's sake,
   The whole o' a' her kin ;
And I will burn for my love's sake,
   Thro' Linkum and thro' Lin.

And mony a bed will I make toom,
   And bower will I make thin ;
And mony a babe shall thole the fire,
   For I may enter in.

Great meen was made for Lady Maisry
   On that hill whare she was slain ;
But mair was for her ain true love,
   On the fields, for he ran brain.

Brown Robyn's Confession.

It fell upon a Wodensday,
  Brown Robyn's men went to sea ;
But they saw neither moon nor sun,
  Nor star-light wi' their e'e.

We'll cast kevels us amang,
  See wha the unhappy man may be ;
The kevel fell on Brown Robyn,
  The master man was hee.

It is nae wonder, said Brown Robyn,
  Altho' I dinna thrive ;
For wi' my mither I had twa bairns,
  And wi' my sister five.

But tie me to a plank o' wude,
  And throw me in the sea ;
And if I sink, ye may bid me sink,
  But if I swim just lat me bee.

They've tyed him to a plank o' wude,
  And thrown him in the sea ;
He didna sink, tho' they bade him sink,
  He swim'd, and they bade lat him bee.

He hadna been into the sea
  An' hour but barely three ;
Till by it came our blessed lady,
  Her dear young son her wi'.

Will ye gang to your men again
  Or, will ye gang wi' me ?
Will ye gang to the high heavens,
  Wi' my dear son and me ?

I winna gang to my men again,
  For they wou'd be fear'd at mee ;
But I wou'd gang to the high heavens,
  Wi' thy dear son and thee.

It's for nae honour ye did to me, Brown Robyn,
  It's for nae guid ye did to mee ;
But a' is for your fair confession,
  You've made upon the sea.

The Three Brothers.

As I walked on a pleasant green,
  'Twas on the first morning of May ;
I heard twa brothers make their moan,
  And hearken'd well what they did say.

The first he gave a grievous sigh,
  And said, Alas ! and wae is me !
We ha'e a brother condemned to death,
  And the very morn must hanged be.

Then out it speaks him little Dick,
   I wat a gude fellow was he;
Had I three men unto mysell,
   Well borrowed shou'd Bell Archie be.

Out it speaks him Johnny Ha,
   A better fellow by far was he;
Ye shall ha'e six men and yoursell,
   And me to bear you companie.

Twa for keepers o' the guard,
   See that to keep it sickerlie;
And twa to come, and twa to gang,
   And twa to speak wi' Bell Archie.

But ye winna gang like men o' weir,
   Nor yet will we like cavalliers;
But we will gang like corn buyers,
   And we'll put brechens on our mares.

Then they are to the jail-house doors,
   And they ha'e tirled at the pin;
Ye sleep ye, wake ye, Bell Archie,
   Quickly rise, lat us come in.

I sleep not aft, I lie not saft,
   Wha's there that knocks and kens my name?
It is your brothers Dick and John;
   Ye'll open the door, lat us come in.

Awa', awa', my brethren dear,
   And ye'll had far awa' frae me ;
If ye be found at jail-house door,
   I fear like dogs they'll gar ye die.

Ohon, alas ! my brother dear,
   Is this the hearkning ye gie to me ?
If ye'll work therein as we thereout,
   Well borrow'd shou'd your body be.

How can I work therein, therein,
   Or yet how can I work thereout,
When fifty tons o' Spanish iron
   Are my fair body round about ?

He put his fingers to the lock,
   I wat he handled them sickerlie ;
And doors of deal, and bands of steel,
   He gart them all in flinders flee.

. He's ta'en the prisoner in his arms,
   And he has kiss'd him cheek and chin ;
Now since we've met, my brother dear,
   There shall be dunts ere we twa twine.

He's ta'en the prisoner on his back,
   And a' his heavy irons tee ;
But and his marie in his hand,
   And straight to Annan gate went he.

But when they came to Annan water,
　　It was roaring like the sea ;
O stay a little, Johnny Ha,
　　Here we can neither fecht nor flee.

O, a refreshment we maun ha'e,
　　We are baith dry and hungry tee ;
We'll gang to Robert's at the mill,
　　It stands upon yon lily lee.

Up in the morning the jailor raise,
　　As soon's 'twas light that he cou'd see ;
Wi' a pint o' wine and a mess sae fine,
　　Into the prison house went he.

When he came to the prison door,
　　A dreary sight he had to see ;
The locks were shot, the doors were broke,
　　And a' the prisoners won free.

Ye'll gae and waken Annan town,
　　Raise up five hundred men and three ;
And if these rascals may be found,
　　I vow like dogs I'll gar them die.

O dinna ye hear proud Annan roar,
　　Mair loud than ever roar'd the sea ?
We'll get the rascals on this side,
　　Sure they can neither fecht nor flee.

Some gar ride, and some gar rin,
   Wi' a' the haste that ye can make;
We'll get them in some tavern house,
   For Annan water they winna take.

As little Dick was looking round,
   All for to see what he could see,
Saw the proud sheriff trip the plain,
   Five hundred men his companie.

O fare ye well, my bonny wife,
   Likewise farewell, my children three;
Fare ye well, ye lands o' Cafield,
   For you again I ne'er will see.

For well I kent ere I came here,
   That Annan water wou'd ruin me;
My horse is young, he'll nae lat ride,
   And in this water I maun die.

Out it speaks him Johnny Ha,
   I wat a gude fellow was he;
O plague upo' your cowardly face,
   The bluntest man I e'er did see.

Gi'e me your horse, take ye my mare,
   The devil drown my mare and thee;
Gi'e me the prisoner on behind,
   And nane will die but he that's fay.

He quickly lap upo' the horse,
    And strait the stirrups siccarlie ;
And jump'd upo' the other side,
    Wi' the prisoner and his irons tee.

The sheriff then came to the bank,
    And heard its roaring like the sea ;
Says, How these men they ha'e got ower,
    It is a marvel unto me.

I wadna venture after them,
    For a' the criminals that I see ;
Nevertheless, now Johnny Ha,
    Throw ower the fetters unto me.

Deil part you and the fetters, he said,
    As lang as my mare needs a shee ;
If she gang barefoot ere they be done,
    I wish an ill death mat ye die.

Awa', awa', now Johnny Ha,
    Your talk to me seems very snell ;
Your mither's been some wild rank witch,
    And you, yoursell, an imp o' hell.

The Maid and Fairy.

O open the door, my honey, my heart,
    O open the door, my ain kind dearie ;
For dinna ye mind upo' the time,
    We met in the wood at the well sae wearie ?

O gi'e me my castick, my dow, my dow,
  O gi'e me my castick, my ain kind dearie ;
For dinna ye mind upo' the time,
  We met in the wood at the well sae weary ?

O gi'e me my brose, my dow, my dow,
  O gi'e me my brose, my ain kind dearie ;
For dinna ye mind upo' the time,
  We met in the wood at the well sae weary ?

O gi'e me my kail, my dow, my dow,
  O gi'e me my kail, my ain kind dearie ;
For dinna ye mind upo' the time,
  We met in the wood at the well sae wearie ?

O lay me down, my dow, my dow,
  O lay me down, my ain kind dearie ;
For dinna ye mind upo' the time,
  We met in the wood at the well sae wearie ?

O woe to you now, my dow, my dow,
  O woe to you now, my wile fause dearie ;
And Oh ! for the time I had you again,
  Plunging the dubs at the well sae wearie !

Young Hunting.

Lady Maisry forth from her bower came,
　And stood on her tower head;
She thought she heard a bridle ring,
　The sound did her heart guid.

She thought it was her first true love,
　Whom she loved ance in time;
But it was her new love, Hunting,
　Come frae the hunting o' the hyn.

Gude morrow, gude morrow, Lady Maisry,
　God make you safe and free!
I'm come to take my last farewell,
　And pay my last visit to thee.

O stay, O stay then, young Hunting,
　O stay with me this night;
Ye shall ha'e cheer, an' charcoal clear,
　And candles burning bright.

Have no more cheer, you lady fair,
　An hour langer for me;
I have a lady in Garmouth town
　I love better than thee.

O if your love be changed, my love,
　Since better canno' be;
Nevertheless, for auld lang syne,
　Ye'll stay this night wi' me.

Silver, silver shall be your wage,
　And gowd shall be your fee ;
And nine times nine into the year,
　Your weed shall changed be.

Will ye gae to the cards or dice,
　Or to a tavern fine ?
Or will ye gae to a table forbye,
　And birl baith beer and wine ?

I winna gang to the cards nor dice,
　Nor to a tavern fine ;
But I will gang to a table forbye,
　And birl baith beer and wine.

Then she has drawn for young Hunting
　The beer but and the wine ;
Till she got him as deadly drunk
　As ony unhallowed swine.

Then she's ta'en out a trusty brand,
　That hang below her gare ;
Then she's wounded him, young Hunting,
　A deep wound and a sair.

Then out it speaks her comrade,
　Being in the companie,
Alas ! this deed that ye hae done,
　Will ruin baith you and me.

Heal well, heal well, you lady Katharine,
   Heal well this deed on me ;
The robes that were shapen for my bodie,
   They shall be sewed for thee.

Tho' I wou'd heal it never sae well,
   And never sae well, said she ;
There is a God above us baith,
   That can baith hear and see.

They booted him and spurred him,
   As he'd been gaun to ride ;
A hunting-horn about his neck,
   A sharp sword by his side.

And they rode on, and farther on
   All the lang summer's tide ;
Until they came to wan water,
   Where a' man ca's it Clyde.

And the deepest pot in Clyde's water,
   And there they flang him in ;
And put a turf on his breast bane,
   To had young Hunting down.

O out it speaks a little wee bird,
   As she sat on the brier ;
Gae hame, gae hame, ye Lady Maisry,
   And pay your maiden's hire.

O I will pay my maiden's hire,
   And hire I'll gi'e to thee;
If ye'll conceal this fatal deed,
   Ye's ha'e gowd for your fee.

Then out it speaks a bonny bird,
   That flew aboon their head;
Keep well, keep well your green claithing,
   Frae ae drap o' his bluid.

O I'll keep well my green claithing
   Frae ae drap o' his bluid;
Better than I'll do your flattering tongue,
   That flutters in your head.

Come down, come down, my bonny bird,
   Light down upon my hand;
For ae gowd feather that's in your wing,
   I wou'd gi'e a' my land.

How shall I come down, how can I come down?
   How shall I come down to thee?
The things ye said to young Hunting,
   The same ye're saying to me.

But it fell out on that same day,
   The king was going to ride;
And he call'd for him, young Hunting,
   For to ride by his side.

Then out it speaks the little young son,
  Sat on the nurse's knee;
It fears me sair, said that young babe,
  He's in bower wi' yon ladie.

Then they ha'e call'd her, Lady Katharine,
  And she sware by the thorn,
That she saw not him, young Hunting,
  Sin' yesterday at morn.

Then they ha'e call'd her, Lady Maisry,
  And she sware by the moon,
That she saw not him, young Hunting,
  Sin' yesterday at noon.

He was playing him at the Clyde's water,
  Perhaps he has fa'en in.
The king he call'd his divers all,
  To dive for his young son.

They div'd in thro' the wan burn-bank,
  Sae did they outthro' the other;
We'll dive nae mair, said these young men,
  Suppose he were our brother.

Then out it spake a little bird,
  That flew aboon their head;
Dive on, dive on, ye divers all,
  For there he lies indeed.

But ye'll leave aff your day diving,
  And ye'll dive in the night;
Thè pot where young Hunting lies in,
  The candles they'll burn bright.

There are twa ladies in yon bower,
  And even in yon ha';
And they ha'e kill'd him, young Hunting,
  And casten him awa'.

They booted him and spurred him,
  As he'd been gaun to ride;
A hunting horn tied round his neck,
  A sharp sword by his side.

The deepest pot o' Clyde's water,
  There they flang him in;
Laid a turf on his breast bane,
  To had young Hunting down.

Now they left aff their day diving,
  And they dived on the night;
The pot that young Hunting lay in,
  The candles were burning bright.

The king he call'd his hewers all,
  To hew down wood and thorn;
For to put up a strong bale-fire,
  These ladies for to burn.

And they ha'e ta'en her, Lady Katharine,
   And they ha'e pitten her in ;
But it wadna light upon her cheek,
   Nor wou'd it on her chin ;
But sang the points o' her yellow hair,
   For healing the deadly sin.

Then they ha'e ta'en her, Lady Maisry,
   And they ha'e put her in.
First it lighted on her cheek,
   And syne upon her chin ;
And sang the points o' her yellow hair,
   And she burnt like keckle-pin.

Blancheflour and Jellyflorice.

There was a maid richly array'd,
   In robes were rare to see ;
For seven years and something mair,
   She serv'd a gay ladie.

But being fond o' a higher place,
   In service she thought lang ;
She took her mantle her about,
   Her coffer by the band.

And as she walk'd by the shore side,
   As blythe's a bird on tree ;
Yet still she gaz'd her round about,
   To see what she could see.

At last she spied a little castle,
 That stood near by the sea ;
She spied it far, and drew it near,
 To that castle went she.

And when she came to that castle,
 She tirled at the pin ;
And ready stood a little wee boy,
 To lat this fair maid in.

O who's the owner of this place,
 O porter boy tell me ?
This place belongs unto a queen
 O' birth and high degree.

She put her hand in her pocket,
 And ga'e him shillings three ;
O porter bear my message well,
 Unto the queen frae me.

The porter's gane before the queen,
 Fell low down on his knee ;
Win up, win up, my porter boy,
 What makes this courtesie ?

I ha'e been porter at your yetts,
 My dame, these years full three ;
But see a ladie at your yetts,
 The fairest my eyes did see.

Cast up my yetts baith wide and braid,
   Lat her come in to me ;
And I'll know by her courtesie,
   Lord's daughter if she be.

When she came in before the queen,
   Fell low down on her knee ;
Service frae you, my dame, the queen,
   I pray you grant it me.

If that service ye now do want,
   What station will ye be ?
Can ye card wool, or spin, fair maid,
   Or milk the cows to me ?

No, I can neither card nor spin,
   Nor cows I canno' milk ;
But sit into a lady's bower,
   And sew the seams o' silk.

What is your name, ye comely dame,
   Pray tell this unto me ?
O Blancheflour, that is my name,
   Born in a strange countrie !

O keep ye well frae Jellyflorice,
   My air dear son is he ;
When other ladies get a gift,
   O' that ye shall get three.

It wasna tald into the bower,
   Till it went thro' the ha',
That Jellyflorice and Blancheflour
   Were grown ower great witha'.

When the queen's maids their visits paid,
   Upo' the gude Yule day;
When other ladies got horse to ride
   She boud take foot and gae.

The queen she call'd her stable groom,
   To come to her right seen;
Says, Ye'll take out yon wild waith steed,
   And bring him to the green.

Ye'll take the bridle frae his head,
   The lighters frae his e'en;
Ere she ride three times round' the cross,
   Her weel days will be dune.

Jellyflorice his true love spy'd,
   As she rade roun' the cross;
And thrice he kiss'd her lovely lips,
   And took her frae her horse.

Gang to your bower, my lily flower,
   For a' my mother's spite;
There's nae other amang her maids,
   In whom I take delight.

Ye are my jewel, and only ane,
   Nane's do you injury;
For ere this-day-month come and gang,
   My wedded wife ye'se be!

Lady Isabel.

'Twas early on a May morning,
   Lady Isabel comb'd her hair;
But little kent she or the morn,
   She would never comb it mair.

'Twas early on a May morning,
   Lady Isabel rang the keys;
But little kent she or the morn,
   A fey woman she was.

Ben it came her step-mother,
   As white's the lily flower;
It's tauld me this day, Isabel,
   You are your father's whore.

O them that tauld you that, mother,
   I wish they ne'er drink wine;
For if I be the same woman,
   My ain sell drees the pine.

And them that's tauld you that, mother,
  I wish they ne'er drink ale ;
For if I be the same woman,
  My ain sell drees the dail.

It may be very well seen, Isabel,
  It may be very well seen,
He buys to you the damask gowns,
  To me the dowie green.

Ye are of age, and I am young,
  And young amo' my flowers ;
The fairer that my claithing be,
  The mair honour is yours.

I hae a love beyond the sea,
  And far ayont the faem ;
For ilka gown my father buys me,
  My ain luve sends me ten.

Come ben, come ben, now Lady Isabel,
  And drink the wine wi' me ;
I hae twa jewels in ae coffer,
  And ane o' them I'll gie.

Stay still, stay still, my mother dear,
  Stay still a little while,
Till I gang into Marykirk,
  Its but a little mile.

VOL. I.   K

When she gaed on to Marykirk,
 And into Mary's quire,
There she saw her ain mother
 Sit in a gowden chair.

O will I leave the lands, mother?
 Or shall I sail the sea?
Or shall I drink this dowie drink,
 That is prepar'd for me?

Ye winna leave the lands, daughter,
 Nor will ye sail the sea,
But ye will drink this dowie drink,
 This woman's prepar'd for thee.

Your bed is made in a better place
 Than ever her's will be,
And ere ye're cauld into the room,
 Ye will be there wi' me.

Come in, come in, now Lady Isabel,
 And drink the wine wi' me ;
I ha'e twa jewels in ae coffer,
 And ane o' them I'll gie.

Stay still, stay still, my mother dear,
 Stay still a little wee,
Till I gang to yon garden green,
 My Maries a' to see.

To some she gae the broach, the broach,
  To some she gae a ring;
But wae befa' her step-mother,
  To her she gae nae thing.

Come in, come in, now Lady Isabel,
  And drink the wine wi' me;
I hae twa jewels in ae coffer,
  And ane o' them I'll gie.

Slowly to the bower she came,
  And slowly enter'd in;
And being full o' courtesie,
  Says, Begin, mother, begin.

She put it till her cheek, her cheek,
  Sae did she till her chin;
Sae did she till her fu' fause lips,
  But never a drap gaed in.

Lady Isabel put it till her cheek,
  Sae did she till her chin;
Sae did she till her rosy lips,
  And the rank poison gaed in.

O take this cup frae me, mother,
  O take this cup frae me;
My bed is made in a better place
  Than ever yours will be.

My bed is in the heavens high,
   Amang the angels fine ;
But yours is in the lowest hell,
   To drie torment and pine.

Nae moan was made for Lady Isabel,
   In bower where she lay dead ;
But a' was for that ill woman,
   In the fields mad she gaed.

Gight's Lady.

First I was Lady o' Black Riggs,
   And then into Kincraigie ;
Now I am the Lady o' Gight,
   And my love he's ca'd Geordie.

I was the mistress o' Pitfan,
   And madam o' Kincraigie ;
But now my name is Lady Anne,
   And I am Gight's own lady.

We courted in the woods o' Gight,
   Where birks and flow'rs spring bonny ;
But pleasures I had never one,
   But sorrows thick and mony.

He never own'd me as his wife,
    Nor honour'd me as his lady ;
But day by day he saddles the grey,
    And rides to Bignet's lady.

When Bignet he got word of that,
    That Gight lay wi' his lady ;
He's casten him in prison strong,
    To ly till lords were ready.

Where will I get a little wee boy,
    That is baith true and steady,
That will run on to bonny Gight,
    And bring to me my lady.

O here am I, a little wee boy,
    That is baith true and steady,
That will run to the yates o' Gight,
    And bring to you your lady.

Ye'll bid her saddle the grey, the grey,
    The brown rode ne'er so smartly ;
Ye'll bid her come to Edinbro' town,
    A' for the life of Geordie.

The night was fair, the moon was clear,
    And he rode by Bevany ;
And stopped at the yates o' Gight,
    Where leaves were thick and mony.

The lady look'd o'er castle wa',
 And dear but she was sorry ;
Here comes a page frae Edinbro' town,
 A' is nae well wi' Geordie.

What news, what news, my little boy ?
 Come tell me soon and shortly ;
Bad news, bad news, my lady, he said,
 They're going to hang your Geordie.

Ye'll saddle to me the grey, the grey
 The brown rade ne'er so smartly ;
And I'll awa' to Edinbro' town,
 Borrow the life o' Geordie.

When she came near to Edinbro' town,
 I wyte she didna tarry ,
But she has mounted her grey steed,
 Aud ridden the queen's berry.

When she came to the boat of Leith,
 I wat she didna tarry ;
She gae the boatman a guinea o' gowd,
 To boat her o'er the ferry.

When she came to the pier o' Leith,
 The poor they were sae many,
She dealt the gowd right liberallie,
 And bade them pray for Geordie.

When she gaed up the tolbooth stair,
　The nobles there were many;
And ilka ane stood hat on head,
　But hat in hand stood Geordie.

She gae a blink out ower them a',
　And three blinks to her Geordie;
But when she saw his een fast bound,
　A swoon fell in this lady.

Whom has he robb'd? What has he stole?
　Or has he killed ony?
Or what's the crime that he has done,
　His foes they are sae mony?

He hasna brunt, he hasna slain,
　He hasna robbed ony;
But he has done another crime,
　For which he will pay dearly.

Then out it speaks Lord Montague,
　(O wae be to his body!)
The day we hang'd young Charles Hay,
　The morn we'll head your Geordie.

Then out it speaks the king himsell,
　Vow but he spake bonny;
Come here young Gight, confess your sins,
　Let's hear if they be mony.

Come here young Gight, confess your sins,
  See ye be true and steady ;
And if your sins they be but sma',
  Then ye'se win wi' your lady.

Nane have I robb'd, nought have I stown,
  Nor have I killed ony ;
But ane o' the king's best brave steeds,
  I sold him in Bevany.

Then out it speaks the king again,
  Dear, but he spake bonny ;
That crime's nae great, for your lady's sake,
  Put on your hat now, Geordie.

Then out it speaks Lord Montague,
  O wae be to his body !
There's guilt appears in Gight's ain face,
  Ye'll cross examine Geordie.

Now since it all I must confess,
  My crimes baith great and mony :
A woman abused, five orphan babes,
  I kill'd them for their money.

Out it speaks the king again,
  And dear but he was sorry ;
Your confession brings confusion,
  Take aff your hat now, Geordie.

Then out it speaks the lady hersell,
   Vow but she was sorry;
Now all my life I'll wear the black,
   Mourn for the death o' Geordie.

Lord Huntly then he did speak out,
   O fair mot fa' his body!
I there will fight doublet alane,
   Or ony thing ails Geordie.

Then out it speaks the king again,
   Vow but he spake bonny;
If ye'll tell down ten thousand crowns,
   Ye'll buy the life o' Geordie.

She spread her mantle on the ground,
   Dear but she spread it bonny;
Some gae her crowns, some ducadoons,
   And some gae dollars mony.
Then she tauld down ten thousand crowns,—
   Put on your hat, my Geordie.

Then out it speaks Lord Montague,
   Wae be to his body!
I wish that Gight wanted the head,
   I might enjoy'd his lady.

Out it speaks the lady hersell,
   Ye need ne'er wish my body;

O ill befa' your wizzen'd snout !
  Would ye compare wi' Geordie ?

When she was in her saddle set,
  Riding the leys sae bonny ;
The fiddle and fleet play'd ne'er sae sweet,
  As she behind her Geordie.

O Geordie, Geordie, I love you well,
  Nae jealousie cou'd move me ;
The birds in air, that fly in pairs,
  Can witness how I love you.

Ye'll call for one, the best o' clerks,
  Ye'll call him soon and shortly ;
As he may write what I indite,
  A' this I've done for Geordie.

He turn'd him right and round about,
  And high, high looked Geordie ;
A finger o' Bignet's lady's hand,
  Is worth a' your fair body.

My lands may a' be masterless,
  My babes may want their mother ;
But I've made a vow, will keep it true,
  I'll be bound to no other.

These words they caus'd a great dispute,
  And proud and fierce grew Geordie !
A sharp dagger he pulled out,
  And pierc'd the heart o's lady.

The lady's dead, and Gight he's fled,
　　And left his lands behind him;
Altho' they searched south and north,
　　There were nane there cou'd find him.

Now a' that liv'd into Black Riggs,
　　And likewise in Kincraigie,
For seven years were clad in black,
　　To mourn for Gight's own lady.

———

The Drowned Lovers.

Willie stands in his stable door,
　　And clapping at his steed;
And looking o'er his white fingers,
　　His nose began to bleed.

Gie corn to my horse, mother,
　　And meat to my young man:
And I'll awa' to Meggie's bower,
　　I'll win ere she lie down.

O bide this night wi' me, Willie,
　　O bide this night wi' me;
The best an' cock o' a' the reest,
　　At your supper shall be.

A' your cocks and a' your reests,
　　I value not a prin;
For I'll awa' to Meggie's bower,
　　I'll win ere she lie down.

Stay this night wi' me, Willie,
 O stay this night wi' me ;
The best an' sheep in a' the flock
 At your supper shall be.

A' your sheep and a' your flocks,
 I value not a prin ;
For I'll awa' to Meggie's bower,
 I'll win ere she lie down.

O an' ye gang to Meggie's bower,
 Sae sair against my will ;
The deepest pot in Clyde's water,
 My malison ye's feel.

The guid steed that I ride upon,
 Cost me thrice thretty pound ;
And I'll put trust in his swift feet,
 To hae me safe to land.

As he rade ower yon high, high hill,
 And down yon dowie den,
The noise that was in Clyde's water
 Wou'd fear'd five huner men.

O roaring Clyde, ye roar ower loud,
 Your streams seem wond'rous strang ;
Make me your wreck as I come back,
 But spare me as I gang.

Then he is on to Meggie's bower,
    And tirled at the pin ;
O sleep ye, wake ye, Meggie, he said,
    Ye'll open, lat me come in.

O wha is this at my bower door,
    That calls me by my name ?
It is your first love, sweet Willie,
    This night newly come hame.

I hae few lovers thereout, thereout,
    As few hae I therein ;
The best an' love that ever I had,
    Was here just late yestreen.

The warstan stable in a' your stables,
    For my puir steed to stand ;
The warstan bower in a' your bowers,
    For me to lie therein :
My boots are fu' o' Clyde's water,
    I'm shivering at the chin.

My barns are fu' o' corn, Willie,
    My stables are fu' o' hay ;
My bowers are fu' o' gentlemen,
    They'll nae remove till day.

O fare-ye-well, my fause Meggie,
    O farewell, and adieu ;
I've gotten my mither's malison,
    This night coming to you.

As he rode ower yon high, high hill,
 And down yon dowie den ;
The rushing that was in Clyde's water,
 Took Willie's cane frae him.

He lean'd him ower his saddle bow,
 To catch his cane again ;
The rushing that was in Clyde's water,
 Took Willie's hat frae him.

He lean'd him ower his saddle bow,
 To catch his hat thro' force ;
The rushing that was in Clyde's water,
 Took Willie frae his horse.

His brither stood upo' the bank,
 Says, Fye, man, will ye drown ?
Ye'll turn ye to your high horse head,
 And learn how to sowm.

How can I turn to my horse head,
 And learn how to sowm ?
I've gotten my mither's malison,
 It's here that I maun drown !

The very hour this young man sank
 Into the pot sae deep,
Up it waken'd his love, Meggie,
 Out o' her drowsy sleep.

Come here, come here, my mither dear,
   And read this dreary dream ;
I dream'd my love was at our yates,
   And nane wad let him in.

Lye still, lye still now, my Meggie,
   Lye still and tak your rest ;
Sin' your true love was at your yates,
   It's but twa quarters past.

Nimbly, nimbly raise she up,
   And nimbly pat she on ;
And the higher that the lady cried,
   The louder blew the win'.

The first an' step that she stepp'd in,
   She stepped to the queet ;
Ohon, alas ! said that lady,
   This water's wond'rous deep.

The next an' step that she wade in,
   She wadit to the knee ;
Says she, I cou'd wide farther in,
   If I my love cou'd see.

The next an' step that she wade in,
   She wadit to the chin ;
The deepest pot in Clyde's water
   She got sweet Willie in.

You've had a cruel mither, Willie,
    And I have had anither ;
But we shall sleep in Clyde's water,
    Like sister an' like brither.

Earl Richard's Daughter.

Earl Richard had but ae daughter,
    A maid o' birth and fame ;
She loved her father's kitchen boy,—
    The greater was her shame.

But she could ne'er her true love see,
    Nor with him could she talk,
In towns where she had wont to go,
    Nor fields where she could walk.

But it fell ance upon a day,
    Her father went from home ;
She's call'd upon the kitchen boy,
    To come and clean her room.

Come sit ye down by me, Willie,
    Come sit ye down by me ;
There's nae a lord in a' the north
    That I can love but thee.

Let never the like be heard, lady,
   Nor let it ever be ;
For if your father get word o' this,
   He will gar hang me hie.

O ye shall ne'er be hang'd, Willie,
   Your blude shall ne'er be drawn ;
I'll lay my life in pledge o' thine,
   Your body's ne'er get wrang.

Excuse me now, my comely dame,
   No langer here I'll stay ;
You know my time is near expir'd,
   And now I must away.

The master-cook will on me call,
   And answered he must be ;
If I am found in bower with thee,
   Great anger will there be.

The master-cook will on you call,
   But shall not answer'd be ;
I'll put you in a higher place
   Than any cook's degree.

I have a coffer full of gold,
   Another of white monie ;
And I will build a bonny ship,
   And set my love to sea.

Silk shall be your sailing clothes,
  Gold yellow in your hair ;
As white like milk are your twa hands,
  Your body neat and fair.

This lady, with her fair speeches,
  She made the boy grow bold ;
And he began to kiss and clap,
  And on his love lay hold.

And she has built a bonny ship,
  Set her love to the sea ;
Seven score o' brisk young men,
  To bear him companie.

Then she's ta'en out a gay gold ring,
  To him she did it gie ;
This will mind you on the ladie, Willie,
  That's laid her love on thee.

Then he's ta'en out a piece of gold,
  And he brake it in two ;
All I have in the world, my dame,
  For love, I give to you.

Now he is to his bonny ship,
  And merrily ta'en the sea ;
The lady lay o'er castle wa',
  The tear blinded her e'e.

They had not sail'd upon the sea
  A week but barely three,
When came a prosperous gale of wind,—
  On Spain's coast landed he.

A lady lay o'er castle wa',
  Beholding dale and down ;
And she beheld the bonny ship
  Come sailing to the town.

Come here, come here, my Maries a',
  Ye see not what I see ;
For here I see the bonniest ship
  That ever sail'd the sea.

In her there is the bravest squire
  That e'er my eyes did see ;
All clad in silk, and rich attire,
  And comely, comely's he.

O busk, O busk, my Maries all,
  O busk and make ye fine ;
And we will on to yon shore side,
  Invite yon squire to dine.

Will ye come up to my castle
  Wi' me, and take your dine ?
And ye shall eat the gude white bread,
  And drink the claret wine.

I thank you for your bread, lady,
    I thank you for your wine ;
I thank you for your kind offer,
    But now I have not time.

I would gi'e all my land, she says,
    Your gay bride were I she ;
And then to live on a small portion,
    Contented I would be.

She's far awa' frae me, lady,
    She's far awa' frae me,
That has my heart a-keeping fast,
    And my love still she'll be.

But ladies they are unconstant,
    When their loves go to sea ;
And she'll be wed ere ye gae back,
    My love, pray stay wi' me.

If she be wed ere I go back,
    And prove sae false to me,
I shall live single all my life,—
    I'll ne'er wed one but she.

Then she's ta'en out a gay gold ring,
    And ga'e him presentlie ;
'Twill mind you on the lady, young man,
    That laid her love on thee.

The ring that's on my mid finger
   Is far dearer to me,
Tho' yours were o' the gude red gold,
   And mine the metal free.

He view'd them all, baith neat and small,
   As they stood on the shore ;
Then hoist the mainsail to the wind,
   Adieu, for evermore !

He had not sail'd upon the sea
   A week but barely three,
Until there came a prosperous gale,
   In Scotland landed he.

But he put paint upon his face,
   And oil upon his hair ;
Likewise a mask above his brow,
   Which did disguise him sair.

Earl Richard lay o'er castle wa',
   Beholding dale and down ;
And he beheld the bonny ship
   Come sailing to the town.

Come here, come here, my daughter dear,
   Ye see not what I see ;
For here I see the bonniest ship
   That ever sail'd the sea.

In her there is the bravest squire
  That e'er my eyes did see ;
O busk, O busk, my daughter dear,
  Come here, come here, to me.

O busk, O busk, my daughter dear,
  O busk, and make ye fine ;
And we will on to the shore side,
  Invite yon squire to dine.

He's far awa' frae me, father,
  He's far awa' frae me,
Who has the keeping o' my heart,
  And I'll wed nane but he.

Whoever has your heart in hand,
  Yon lad's the match for thee ;
And he shall come to my castle
  This day, and dine wi' me.

Will ye come up to my castle
  With me, and take your dine ?
And ye shall eat the gude white bread,
  And drink the claret wine.

Yes, I'll come up to your castle
  With you, and take my dine ;
For I would give my bonny ship
  Were your fair daughter mine.

I would give all my lands, he said,
  That your bride she would be ;
Then to live on a small portion,
  Contented would I be.

As they gaed up from yon sea strand,
  And down the bowling green,
He drew the mask out o'er his face,
  For fear he should be seen.

He's done him down from bower to bower,
  Likewise from bower to ha' ;
And there he saw that lady gay,
  The flower out o'er them a'.

He's ta'en her in his arms twa,
  And hail'd her courteouslie ;
Excuse me, sir, there's no strange man
  Such freedom use with me.

Her father turn'd him round about,
  A light laugh then gave he ;
Stay, I'll retire a little while,
  Perhaps you may agree.

Now Willie's ta'en a gay gold ring,
  And gave her presentlie ;
Says, Take ye that, ye lady fair,
  A love token from me.

O got ye't on the sea sailing ?
  Or got ye't on the sand ?
Or got ye't on the coast of Spain,
  Upon a dead man's hand ?

Fine silk it was his sailing clothes,
  Gold yellow was his hair ;
It would ha'e made a hale heart bleed
  To see him lying there.

He was not dead as I pass'd by,
  But no remeid could be ;
He gave me this token to bear
  Unto a fair ladie.

And by the marks he has descryv'd,
  I'm sure that you are she ;
So take this token of free will,
  For him you'll never see.

In sorrow she tore her mantle,
  With care she tore her hair ;
Now since I've lost my own true love,
  I'll ne'er love young men mair.

He drew the mask from off his face,
  The lady sweetly smiled ;
Awa', awa', ye fause Willie,
  How have you me beguiled ?

Earl Richard he went thro' the ha',
  The wine glass in his hand ;
But little thought his kitchen boy,
  Was heir o'er a' his land.

But this she kept within her heart,
  And never told to one ;
Until nine months they were expir'd
  That her young son came home.

She told it to her father dear ;
  He said, Daughter, well won ;
You've married for love, not for gold,
  Your joys will ne'er be done.

Willie and Lady Maisry.

Sweet Willie was a widow's son,
  And milk-white was his weed:
It sets him weel to bridle a horse,
  And better to saddle a steed, my dear,
  And better to saddle a steed.

But he is on to Maisry's bower door,
  And tirled at the pin ;
Ye sleep ye, wake ye, Lady Maisry,
  Ye'll open, let me come in, my dear,
  Ye'll open, let me come in.

O who is this at my bower door,
  Sae well that knows my name ?
It is your ain true love, Willie,
  If ye love me, lat me in, my dear,
  If ye love me, lat me in.

Then huly, huly raise she up,
  For fear o' making din ;
Then in her arms lang and bent,
  She caught sweet Willie in, my dear,
  She caught sweet Willie in.

She lean'd her low down to her toe,
  To loose her true love's sheen ;
But cauld, cauld were the draps o' bleed,
  Fell fae his trusty brand, my dear,
  Fell fae his trusty brand.

What frightfu' sight is that, my love ?
  A frightfu' sight to see ;
What bluid is this on your sharp brand,
  O may ye not tell me, my dear ?
  O may ye not tell me ?

As I came thro' the woods this night,
  The wolf maist worried me ;
O shou'd I slain the wolf, Maisry ?
  Or shou'd the wolf slain me, my dear ?
  Or shou'd the wolf slain me ?

They hadna kiss'd nor love clapped,
   As lovers when they meet,
Till up it starts her auld father
   Out o' his drowsy sleep, my dear,
   Out o' his drowsy sleep.

O what's become o' my house cock
   Sae crouse at ane did craw?
I wonder as much at my bold watch,
   That's nae shooting ower the wa', my dear;
   That's nae shooting ower the wa.

My gude house cock, my only son,
   Heir ower my land sae free;
If ony ruffian hae him slain,
   High hanged shall he be, my dear,
   High hanged shall he be?

Then he's on to Maisry's bower door,
   And tirled at the pin;
Ye sleep ye, wake ye, daughter Maisry,
   Ye'll open, lat me come in, my dear,
   Ye'll open, lat me come in.

Between the curtains and the wa',
   She row'd her true love then;
And huly went she to the door,
   And let her father in, my dear,
   And let her father in.

What's become o' your Maries, Maisry,
  Your bower it looks sae teem?
What's become o' your green claithing?
  Your beds they are sae thin, my dear,
  Your beds they are sae thin.

Gude forgive you, father, she said,
  I wish ye be't for sin;
Sae aft as ye hae dreaded me,
  But never found me wrong, my dear,
  But never found me wrong.

He turn'd him right and round about,
  As he'd been gaun awa';
But sae nimbly as he slippet in,
  Behind a screen sae sma', my dear,
  Behind a screen sae sma'.

Maisry thinking a' dangers past,
  She to her love did say;
Come, love, and take your silent rest,
  My auld father's away, my dear,
  My auld father's away!

Then baith lock'd in each other's arms,
  They fell full fast asleep;
When up it starts her auld father,
  And stood at their bed feet, my dear,
  And stood at their bed feet.

I think I hae the villain now,
   That my dear son did slay;
But I shall be reveng'd on him,
   Before I see the day, my dear,
   Before I see the day.

Then he's drawn out a trusty brand,
   And stroak'd it o'er a stray;
And thro' and thro' sweet Willie's middle
   He's gart cauld iron gae, my dear,
   He's gart cauld iron gae.

Then up it waken'd Lady Maisry
   Out o' her drowsy sleep;
And when she saw her true love slain,
   She straight began to weep, my dear,
   She straight began to weep.

O gude forgie you, now father, she said,
   I wish ye be't for sin;
For I never lov'd a love but ane,
   In my arms ye've him slain, my dear,
   In my arms ye've him slain.

This night he's slain my gude bold watch,
   Thirty stout men and twa;
Likewise he's slain your ae brother,
   To me was worth them a', my dear,
   To me was worth them a'.

If he has slain my ae brither,
  Himsell had a' the blame ;
For mony a day he plots contriv'd,
  To hae sweet Willie slain, my dear,
  To hae sweet Willie slain.

And tho' he's slain your gude bold watch,
  He might hae been forgien ;
They came on him in armour bright,
  When he was but alane, my dear,
  When he was but alane.

Nae meen was made for this young knight,
  In bower where he lay slain ;
But a' was for sweet Maisry bright,
  In fields where she ran brain, my dear,
  In fields where she ran brain.

Clerk Sandy.

Clerk Sandy and a lady gay
  Were walking in the garden green ;
And great and heavy was the love
  That hae befa'en these twa between.

A bed, a bed, said Clerk Sandy,
  A bed, my love, for you and me ;
O never a foot, said the lady gay,
  Till ance that we twa married be.

My seven brithers will come in,
   And a' their torches burning bright ;
They'll say, We hae but ae sister,
   And here she's lying wi' a knight.

Ye'll take my brand I bear in hand,
   And wi' the same ye'll lift the gin ;
Then ye may swear and save your oath,
   That ye ne'er let Clerk Sandy in.

Ye'll take that kurchie on your head,
   And wi' the same tie up your een ;
And ye will swear and save your oath,
   Ye saw not Sandy sin' yestreen.

Ye'll lift me in your arms twa,
   And carry me unto your bed ;
Then ye may swear and save your oath,
   Clerk Sandy in your bower ne'er tread.

She's ta'en the brand he bare in hand,
   And wi' the same lifted the gin ;
It was to swear and save her oath,
   She never loot Clerk Sandy in.

She's ta'en the kurchie frae her head,
   And wi' the same tied up her een ;
It was to swear and save her oath,
   She saw not Sandy sin' yestreen.

She's ta'en him in her arms twa,
   And she's carried him to her bed ;
It was to swear and save her oath,
   Clerk Sandie in her bower ne'er tread.

They hadna kiss'd, nor love clapped,
   Like other lovers when they meet,
Till in a quarter's space and less,
   These two lovers fell sound asleep.

Then in it came her seven brothers,
   And a' their torches burning bright ;
They said, we hae but ae sister,
   And here she's lying wi' a knight.

O, out it speaks the first o' them,
   We will awa' and lat them be ;
Then out it speaks the second o' them,
   His father has nae mair but he.

Out it speaks the third o' them,
   For he was standing on the birk ;
Nae sweeter cou'd twa lovers lye,
   Tho' they'd been married in a kirk.

Then out it speaks the fourth o' them,
   Mair fair and lovely is his buke ;
Our sister dear we cannot blame,
   Altho' in him she pleasure took.

Then out it speaks the fifth o' them,
  It were a sin to do them ill;
Then out it spake the sixth o' them,
  It's hard a sleeping man to kill.

But out it speaks the seventh o' them,
  (I wish an ill death mat he dee!)
I wear the sharp brand by my side,
  That soon shall gar Clerk Sandy die.

Then he's ta'en out his trusty brand,
  And he has stroak'd it ower a strae ·
And thro' and thro' Clerk Sandy's middle
  I wat he's gart it come and gae.

The lady slept by her love's side
  Until the dawning o' the day;
But what was dune she naething knew,
  For when she wak'd these words did say,—

Awake, awake, now Clerk Sandy,
  Awake, and turn you unto me;
Ye're nae sae keen's ye were at night,
  When you and I met on the lee.

O, then she call'd her chamber-maid
  To bring her coal and candle seen;
I fear Clerk Sandy's dead eneuch,
  I had a living man yestreen.

They hae lifted his body up,
  They hae searched it round and round,
And even anent his bonny heart,
  Discovered the deadly wound.

She wrung her hands and tore her hair,
  And wrung her hands most bitterlie;
This is my fause brothers, I fear,
  This night hae used this crueltie.

But I will do for my love's sake
  Wou'd nae be done by ladies rare;
For seven years shall hae an end,
  Or e'er a kame gang in my hair.

O, I will do for my love's sake
  What other ladies wou'd think lack;
For seven years shall hae an end,
  Or e'er I wear but dowie black.

And I will do for my love's sake
  What other ladies woudna thole;
Seven years shall hae an end,
  Or e'er a shoe gang on my sole.

In it came her father dear,
  And he was belted in a brand;
Sae softly as he trad the floor,
  And in her bower did stately stand.

Says, Hold your tongue, my daughter dear,
   And ye'll lat a' your mourning be ;
I'll wed you to a higher match,
   Or e'er his father's son cou'd be.

Wed well, wed well your seven sons,
   I wish ill wedded they may be ;
Sin' they hae kill'd him, Clerk Sandy,
   For wedded shall I never be.

His corpse was laid in the cauld clay,
   The bells went tinkling thro' the town ;
Alas! alas! said the lady gay,
   That e'er I heard that waefu' soun' !

When she had sitten intill her bower
   A twalmonth lang and weary day ;
Even below her bower window,
   She heard a ghaist to knock an' cry.

She says, ye're thief or bauld robber,
   Or biggin come to burn or brake ;
Or are you ony masterfu' man,
   That is come seeking ony make ?

I am not thief nor bauld robber,
   Nor bigging come to burn nor brake ;
Nor am I ony masterfu' man
   That is come seeking ony make ;
But I'm Clerk Sandy, your first love,
   And wants wi' you to speak again.

Gin ye're Clerk Sandy, my first love,
　　And wants wi' me to speak again ;
Tell me some o' the love tokens
　　That you and I had last between.

O mind not ye, ye gay lady,
　　Sin' last I was in bower wi' thee,
That in it came your seven brethren,
　　The youngest gart me sairly dree ?
Then sigh'd, and said the gay lady,
　　Sae true a tale as ye tell me.

Sae painfully she clam the wa',
　　She clam the wa' up after him ;
'Twas not for want of stockings nor sheen,
　　But hadna time to put them on ;
And in the midst o' gude greenwood
　　'Twas there she lost the sight o' him.

The lady sat, and mourning there,
　　Until she coudna weep nae mair ;
At length the cloks and wanton flies,
　　They biggit in her yellow hair.

O had your peace, my dearest dear,
　　For I am come to mak' you wise ;
Or this night nine nights come aud gang,
　　We baith shall be in Paradise !

Willie and Fair Burd Ann.

Willie cou'd neither read nor write,
　　Annie cou'd neither card nor spin ;
But he is on to Edinburgh town,
　　To learn to be a gay merchant.

A huudred pounds o' pennies round,
　　His love rowed up in servet sma' ;
Says, Take ye that, my love, Willie,
　　It will begin your pack witha'.

When ye are gane to Edinburgh town,
　　And has your trade in your right hand,
O come ye back some misty night,
　　And steal awa' your ain burd Ann.

When Willie had gane to Edinburgh town,
　　And had his trade in his right han' ;
Then he came back in a misty night,
　　And stole awa' his ain burd Ann.

When they were got on gude ship board,
　　As they lay there a while wind-bound ;
Annie minded on a glove she left,
　　And Willie on a gude grey hound.

But now to have his grey hound fetched,
　　Willie jumped upon the land ;
The wind blew fair, the ship did sail,—
　　They had awa' his dear burd Ann.

Annie stood upon the deck,
   And waved her fan into her han';
Return, return, sweet Willie, she said,
   They're taking awa' your ain burd Ann.

Ye've lost the thing ye'll never get,
   Ye've lost the thing ye'll never find;
Ye've lost the thing ye'll never get,
   Your true love for a grey bitch hound.

Willie stood upon the shore,
   And waved his hat into his han';
Stay still, stay still, ye bold mariners,
   Do not hae awa' my dear burd Ann.

Seven days Ann sailed the sea,
   And seven Willie ga'ed by lan',
But a true woman Ann was aye,
   And a true woman her he fan'.

The Enchanted Ring.

In Lauderdale I chanc'd to walk,
   And heard a lady's moan,
Lamenting for her dearest dear,
   And aye she cried, Ohon!

Sure never a maid that e'er drew breath
  Had harder fate than me ;
I'd never a lad but one on earth,
  They forced him to the sea.

The ale shall ne'er be brewin o' malt,
  Neither by sea nor land,
That ever mair shall cross my hause,
  Till my love comes to hand.

A handsome lad wi' shoulders broad,
  Gold yellow was his hair ;
None of our Scottish youths on earth
  That with him could compare.

She thought her love was gone to sea,
  And landed in Bahome ;
But he was in a quiet chamber,
  Hearing his lady's moan.

Why make ye all this moan, lady ?
  Why make ye all this moan ?
For I'm deep sworn on a book,
  I must go to Bahome.

Traitors false for to subdue,
  O'er seas I'll make me boun' ;
That have trepan'd our kind Scotchmen,
  Like dogs to ding them down.

Weell take this ring, this royal thing,
　　Whose virtue is unknown ;
As lang's this ring's your body on,
　　Your blood shall ne'er be drawn.

But if this ring shall fade or stain,
　　Or change to other hue,
Come never mair to fair Scotland
　　If ye're a lover true.

Then this couple they did part
　　With a sad heavy moan ;
The wind was fair, the ship was rare,
　　They landed in Bahome.

But in that place they had not been
　　A month but barely one,
Till they look'd on his gay gold ring,
　　And riven was the stone.

Time after this was not expir'd
　　A month but scarcely three,
Till black and ugly was the ring,
　　And stone was burst in three.

Fight on, fight on, you merry men all,
　　With you I'll fight no more ;
I will gang to some holy place,
　　Pray to the King of Glore.

Then to the chapel he is gone,
  And knelt most piteouslie ;
For seven days and seven nights,
  Till blood ran frae his knee.

Ye'll take my jewels that's in Bahome,
  And deal them liberallie.
To young that cannot, and old that mannot,
  The blind that does not see.

Give maist to women in child-bed laid,
  Can neither fecht nor flee ;
I hope she's in the heavens high,
  That died for love of me.

The knights they wrang their white fingers,
  The ladies tore their hair ;
The women that ne'er had children born,
  In swoon they down fell there.

But in what way the knight expir'd,
  No tongue will e'er declare ;
So this doth end my mournful song,
  From me ye'll get nae mair.

Broom o' the Cowdenknowes.

'Twas on a misty day, a fair maiden gay,
  Went out to the Cowdenknowes ;

Lang, lang she thought ere her ewes wou'd bught,
  Wi' her pail for to milk the ewes.
Chorus—O, the broom, the bonny, bonny broom,
      The broom o' the Cowdenknowes ;
      And aye sae sweet as the lassie sang,
      In the ewe-bught milking her ewes.

And aye as she sang, the greenwoods rang,
  Her voice was sae loud and shrill ;
They heard the voice o' this well-far'd maid,
  At the other side o' the hill.
    O, the broom, the bonny, bonny broom, &c,

My mother she is an ill woman,
  And an ill woman is she ;
Or than she might have got some other maid
  To milk her ewes without me.
        O, the broom, &c.

My father was ance a landed laird,
  As mony mair have been ;
But he held on the gambling trade
  Till a's free lands were dune.
        O, the broom, &c.

My father drank the brandy and beer,
  My mother the wine sae red ;
Gars me, poor girl, gang maiden lang,
  For the lack o' tocher guid,
        O, the broom, &c.

There was a troop o' merry gentlemen
   Came riding alang the way ;
And one o' them drew the ewe-bughts unto,
   At the voice of this lovely may.
         O, the broom, &c.

O well may you sing, my well-far'd maid,
   And well may you sing, I say ;
For this is a mirk and a misty night,
   And I've ridden out o' my way.
         O, the broom, &c.

Ride on, ride on, young man, she said,
   Ride on the way ye ken ;
But keep frae the streams o' the Rock-river,
   For they run proud and vain.
         O, the broom, &c.

Ye winna want boys for meat, kind sir,
   And ye winna want men for fee ;
It sets not us that are young women,
   To show young men the way.
         O, the broom, &c.

O winna ye pity me, fair maid ?
   O winna ye pity me ?
O winna ye pity my poor steed,
   Stands trembling at yon tree ?
         O, the broom, &c.

Ride on, ride on, ye rank rider,
　　Your steed's baith stout and strang ;
For out o' the ewe-bught I winna come,
　　For fear that ye do me wrang.
　　　　　O, the broom, &c.

For well ken I by your high-coll'd hat,
　　And by your gay gowd ring,
That ye are the Earl o' the Rock-rivers,
　　That beguiles a' our young women.
　　　　　O, the broom, &c.

O I'm not the Earl o' the Rock-rivers,
　　Nor ever thinks to be ;
But I am ane o' his finest knights,
　　Rides aft in his companie.
　　　　　O, the broom, &c.

I know you well by your lamar beads,
　　And by your merry winking e'e,
That ye are the maid o' the Cowdenknowes,
　　And may very well seem to be.
　　　　　O, the broom, &c.

He's ta'en her by the milk-white hand,
　　And by the grass-green sleeve ;
He's laid her down by the ewe-bught wa',
　　At her he spiered nae leave.
　　　　　O, the broom, &c.

When he had got his wills o' her,
   And his wills he had ta'en ;
He lifted her up by the middle sae sma',
   Says, Fair maid, rise up again.
          O, the broom, &c.

Then he has ta'en out a siller kaim,
   Kaim'd down her yellow hair ;
Says, Fair maid take that, keep it for my sake,
   Case frae me ye never get mair.
          O, the broom, &c.

Then he put his hand in his pocket,
   And gi'en her guineas three ;
Says, Take that, fair maiden, till I return,
   'Twill pay the nurse's fee.
          O, the broom, &c.

Then he lap on his milk-white steed,
   And he rade after his men ;
And a' that they did say to him,
   Dear master, ye've tarried lang.
          O, the broom, &c.

I've ridden east, I've ridden west,
   And over the Cowdenknowes ;
But the bonniest lass that e'er I did see,
   Was i' the ewe-bught milking her ewes.
          O, the broom, &c.

She's ta'en her milk-pail on her head,
    And she gaed singing hame ;
But a' that her auld father did say,
    Daughter, ye've tarried lang.
Chorus.—O, the broom, the bonny, bonny broom,
        The broom o' the Cowdenknowes,
     Aye sae sair's I may rue the day,
        In the ewe-bughts milking my ewes.

O this is a mirk and a misty night,
    O father, as ye may see ;
The ewes they ran skipping over the knowes,
    And they woudna bught in for me.
        O, the broom, &c.

Before that he'd ta'en the lamb that he took,
    I rather he'd ta'en other three ;
When twenty weeks were come and gane,
    And twenty weeks and three,
The lassie's colour grew pale and wan,
    And she longed this knight to see.
        O, the broom, &c.

Says, Wae to the fox came amo' our flock,
    I wish he had ta'en them a',
Before that he'd ta'en frae me what he took ;
    It's occasion'd my downfa'.
        O, the broom, &c.

It fell ance upon a time,
   She was ca'ing hame her kye,
There came a troop o' merry gentlemen,
   And they wyled the bonny lassie by.
         O, the broom, &c.

But one o' them spake as he rode past,
   Says, Who owes the bairn ye are wi' ?
A little she spake, but thought wi' hersell,
   Perhaps to ane as gude as thee.
         O, the broom, &c.

O then she did blush as he did pass by,
   And dear but she thought shame ;
And all that she did say to him,
   Sir, I have a husband at hame.
         O, the broom, &c.

Ye lie, ye lie, ye well-far'd maid,
   Sae loud as I hear you lie ;
For dinna ye mind yon misty night,
   Ye were in the bught wi' me ?
     O, the broom, the bonny, bonny broom,
       The broom o' the Cowdenknowes ;
     Aye say sweet as I heard you sing,
       In the ewe-bughts milking your ewes.

O well do I mind, kind sir, she said,
   As ye rode over the hill,

Ye took frae me my maidenhead,
　Fell sair against my will.
　　　O, the broom, the bonny, bonny broom,
　　　　The broom o' the Cowdenknowes ;
　　　And aye sae sair as I rue the day,
　　　　I met you milking my ewes.

And aye as ye spake, ye lifted your hat,
　Ye had a merry winking e'e ;
I ken you well to be the man,
　Then kind sir, O pity me.
　　　　　　O, the broom, &c.

Win up, win up, fair maiden, he said,
　Nae langer here ye'll stay ;
This night ye'se be my wedded wife,
　Without any more delay.
　　　　　　O, the broom, &c.

He lighted aff his milk-white steed,
　And set the lassie on ;
Ca' in your kye, auld man, he did say,
　She'll ne'er ca' them in again.
　　　　　　O, the broom, &c.

I'm the Earl o' the Rock-rivers,
　Ha'e fifty ploughs and three ;
And am sure I've chosen the fairest maid,
　That ever my eyes did see.
　　　　　　O, the broom, &c.

Then he stripped her o' the robes o' grey,
   Dress'd her in the robes o' green :
And when she came to her lord's ha',
   They took her to be some queen.
     O the broom, the bonny, bonny broom,
      The broom o' the Cowdenknowes ;
     And aye sae sweet as the bonny lassie sang,
      That ever she milked the ewes !

Proud Maitland.

Come choose a fere, my daughter dear,
   As lang as ye hae me ;
For when I'm dead and laid in grave,
   There's none will care for thee.

This pleases me, my father dear,
   The words I hear you say ;
For if I getna proud Maitland,
   I'll die before my day.

O there are lords that courted me,
   And knights o' high degree ;
My love was laid on proud Maitland,
   From all that I do see.

Her father wrote a broad letter,
   And seal'd it with his hand ;
And sent it on to proud Maitland,
   As fast as boy could gang.

O when he look'd the letter on,
   A light laugh then ga'e he ;
I'm sure this is the first woman,
   That's laid her love on me.

O busk, O busk, my merry men a',
   O busk and gang wi' me ;
And we will on to Morrice dale,
   That lady for to see.

When he was in his saddle set,
   A tall young man was he ;
About five hundred wall-wight men,
   To bear him companie.

Her father lay ower castle wa',
   Beholding dale and down ;
And saw proud Maitland and his men
   Come riding to the town.

He turn'd about and ga'e a shout
   O who are all these I see ?
I'm sure gin a' these get their dine,
   There will be nae guid o' me !

The men maun get baith boil'd and roast,
  Their horses corn and hay ;
And gin I hae wared a' this cost,
  My debts I'll never pay.

Proud Maitland muster'd all his men,
  And bade them stand a' still ;
Till he is on his journey gone,
  Out o'er the Pentland hill.

And when he came to Morrice dale,
  A loud shout then gae he ;
Are ye the lady that lives here ?
  Or what's your wills wi' me ?

There are mony gude lords courted me,
  And barons o' high degree ;
But ye are the man my love's fix'd on,
  By a' that I do see.

I'll put smiths in your smithy,
  To shoe for you a steed ;
And I'll put tailors in your bower,
  To shape for you a weed.

I'll put cooks in your kitchen,
  And butlers in your ha' ;
And horse-grooms in your stable there,
  To answer when you ca'.

O wae mat worth you, jelly Janet,
   Ye've learn'd to court, I see ;
Your mither was never to your father
   As married woman shou'd be.

Down below my father's garden,
   There grows an apple tree,
And three upon the sunny side,
   But it's worth a' the three.
Mony ill cow's had a gude calf,
   Sae has my mither o' me.

O wae mat worth you, jelly Janet,
   If ye do not as you say ;
If that I wed you with a ring,
   I'll gar you rue the day.

Wi' tows I'll tie you to a stake,
   And bind you wi' a chain ;
And ilka day I'll beat your dog,
   Your father did ne'er incline.

Lord Darlington.

O we were seven brave sisters,
   Five of us died wi' child ;
And nane but you and I, Maisry,
   So we'll gae maidens mild.

O had your tongue, now Lady Margaret,
   Let a' your folly be ;
I'll gar you keep your true promise,
   To the lad ayont the sea.

O there is neither lord nor knight
   My love shall ever won,
Except it be Lord Darlington,
   And here he winna come.

But when the hour o' twall was past,
   And near the hour o' one,
Lord Darlington came to the yetts,
   Wi' thirty knights and ten.

Then he has wedded Lady Margaret,
   And brought her o'er the sea ;
And there was nane that lived on earth,
   Sae happy as was she.

But when nine months were come and gane,
   Strong travailling took she ;
And nae physician in the land
   Could ease her maladie.

Where will I get a little wee boy
   Will won baith meat and fee,
That will gae on to Seaton's yetts,
   Bring my mother to me ?

O here am I, a little wee boy,
   That will won meat and fee ;
That will gae on to Seaton's yetts,
   And bring your mother to thee.

Then he is on to Seaton's yetts,
   As fast as gang could he ;
Says, Ye must come to Darlington,
   Your daughter for to see.

But when she came to Darlington,
   Where there was little pride,
The scobbs were in the lady's mouth,
   The sharp sheer in her side.

Darlington stood on the stair,
   And gart the gowd rings flee ;
My ha's and bowers, and a' shall gae waste,
   If my bonny love die for me.

O had your tongue, Lord Darlington,
   Let a' your folly be ;
I boor the bird within my sides,
   I'll suffer her to die.

But him that marries my daughter,
   I think he is a fool ;
If he marries her at Candlemas,
   She'll be frae him ere Yule.

I had seven ance in companie,
   This night I go my lane;
And when I come to Clyde's water,
   I wish that I may drown.

Blue Flowers and Yellow.

O Willie, my son, what makes you sae sad?
   As the sun shines over the valley;
I lye sarely sick for the love of a maid,
   Amang the blue flowers and the yellow.

Were she an heiress or lady sae free,
   As the sun shines over the valley,
That she will take no pity on thee,
   Amang the blue flowers and the yellow?

O Willie, my son, I'll learn you a wile,
   As the sun shines over the valley;
How this fair maid ye may beguile,
   Amang the blue flowers and the yellow.

Ye'll gi'e the principal bellman a groat,
   As the sun shines over the valley;
And ye'll gar him cry your dead lyke wake
   Amang the blue flowers and the yellow.

Then he gae the principal bellman a groat,
 As the sun shines over the valley ;
He bade him cry his dead lyke wake,
 Amang the blue flowers and the yellow.

This maiden she stood till she heard it a',
 As the sun shines over the valley ;
And down frae her cheeks the tears did fa',
 Amang the blue flowers and the yellow.

She is hame to her father's ain bower,
 As the sun shines over the valley ;
I'll gang to yon lyke wake ae single hour,
 Amang the blue flowers and the yellow.

Ye must take with you, your ain brither John,
 As the sun shines over the valley ;
It's not meet for maidens to venture alone,
 Amang the blue flowers and the yellow.

I'll not take with me my brither John,
 As the sun shines over the valley ;
But I'll gang along, myself all alone,
 Amang the blue flowers and the yellow.

When she came to young Willie's yate,
 As the sun shines over the valley ;
His seven brithers were standing thereat,
 Amang the blue flowers and the yellow.

Then they did conduct her into the ha',
　　As the sun shines over the valley ;
Amang the weepers and merry mourners a',
　　Amang the blue flowers and the yellow.

When she lifted up the covering sae red,
　　As the sun shines over the valley ;
With melancholy countenance to look on the dead,
　　Amang the blue flowers and the yellow ;

He's taen her in his arms, laid her 'gainst the wa',
　　As the sun shines over the valley ;
Says, Lye ye here, fair maid, till day,
　　Amang the blue flowers and the yellow.

O spare me, O spare me, but this single night,
　　As the sun shines over the valley ;
And let me gang hame a maiden sae bright,
　　Amang the blue flowers and the yellow.

Tho' all your kin were about your bower,
　　As the sun shines over the valley ;
Ye shall not be a maiden ae single hour,
　　Amang the blue flowers and the yellow.

Fair maid, ye came here without a convoy,
　　As the sun shines over the valley ;
But ye shall return wi' a horse and a boy,
　　Amang the blue flowers and the yellow.

Ye came here a maiden sae mild,
   As the sun shines over the valley;
But ye shall gae hame a wedded wife with child,
   Amang the blue flowers and the yellow.

Jean o' Bethelnie's Love

FOR SIR G. GORDON.

There were four-and-twenty ladies,
   Dined i' the queen's ha';
And Jean o' Bethelnie
   Was the flower o' them a'.

Four-and-twenty gentlemen
   Rode thro' Banchory fair;
But bonny Glenlogie,
   Was the flower that was there.

Young Jean at a window,
   She chanced to sit nigh;
And upon Glenlogie,
   She fixed an eye.

She call'd on his best man,
   Unto him did say;—
O what is that knight's name?
   Or where does he stay?

He's of the noble Gordons,
  Of great birth and fame;
He stays at Glenlogie,
  Sir George is his name!

Then she wrote a broad letter,
  And wrote it in haste ;
To send to Glenlogie,
  She thought it was best.

Says, O brave Glenlogie,
  Unto me be kind ;
I've laid my love on you,
  And told you my mind.

Then reading the letter,
  As he stood on the green ;
Says, I leave you to judge, sirs,
  What does women mean ?

Then turn'd about sprightly,
  As the Gordons do a' ;
Lay not your love on me,
  I'm promised awa'.

When she heard this answer,
  Her heart was like to break,
That she laid her love on him,
  And him so ungrate.

Then she call'd on her maidens,
  To lay her to bed ;
And take her fine jewels,
  And lay them aside.

My seals and my signets,
  No more shall I crave ;
But linen and trappin,
  A chest and a grave.

Her father stood by her,
  Possessed with fear ;
To see his dear daughter,
  Possessed with care.

Says, Hold your tongue, Jeanie,
  Let all your folly be ;
I'll wed you to Dumfedline,
  He is better than he.

O hold your tongue, father,
  And let me alane ;
If I getna Glenlogie,
  I'll never have ane.

His bonny jimp middle,
  His black rolling eye ;
If I getna Glenlogie,
  I'm sure I shall die.

But her father's old chaplain,
  A man of great skill;
He wrote a broad letter,
  And penned it well.

Saying, O brave Glenlogie,
  Why must it be so ?
A maid's love laid on you,
  Shall she die in her woe ?

Then reading the letter,
  His heart was like to break,
That such a leal virgin
  Should die for his sake.

Then he call'd on his footman,
  And likewise his groom;
Says, Get my horse saddled
  And bridled soon.

Before the horse was saddled,
  And brought to the yate;
Bonnie Glenlogie,
  Was five miles on foot.

When he came to Bethelnie,
  He saw nothing there,
But weeping and wailing,
  Vexation and care.

Then out spake her father,
  With the tear in his e'e;

You're welcome, Glenlogie,
   You're welcome to me.

If ye make me welcome,
   As welcome's ye say ;
Ye'll show me the chamber,
   Where Jeannie does lay.

Then one o' her maidens
   Took him by the hand ;
To show him the chamber
   Where Jeannie lay in.

Before that she saw him,
   She was pale and wan ;
But when she did see him,
   She grew ruddy again.

O turn, bonny Jeannie,
   Turn you to your side ;
For I'll be the bridegroom,
   And ye'll be the bride.

When Jeannie was married,
   Her tocher down tauld ;
Bonny Jean o' Bethelnie,
   Was fifteen years auld.

The Holy Nunnery.

Fair Annie had a costly bower,
   Well built wi' lime and stane ;

And Willie came to visit her,
  Wi' the light o' the meen.

When he came to Annie's bower door,
  He tirled at the pin ;
O sleep ye, wake ye, fair Annie,
  Ye'll open, lat me come in.

O never a fit, says fair Annie,
  Till I your errand ken.
My father's vow'd a vow, Annie,
  I'll tell you when I'm in.

My father's vowed a rash vow,
  I darena marry thee ;
My mither's vowed anither vow,
  My bride ye'se never be.

If ye had tauld me that, Willie,
  When we began to woo ;
There was naithing in this warld wide
  Shou'd drawn my love to you.

A nun, a nun, said fair Annie,
  A nun will I be then,
A priest, a priest, said sweet Willie,
  A priest will I be syne.

She is gane to her father,
  (For mither she had nane ;)
And she is on to her father,
  To see if she'd be a nun.

An asking, asking, father dear,
   An asking ye'll grant me ;
That's to get to the holy Nunnery,
   And there to live or die.

Your asking's nae sae great, daughter,
   But granted it shall be ;
For ye'se won to the holy Nunnery,
   There to live or die.

Then they gaed on, and farther on,
   Till they came to the yate ;
And there they spied a maiden porter,
   Wi' gowd upon her hat.

An asking, asking, maiden porter,
   An asking ye'll grant me ;
If I'll won to the holy Nunnery,
   There to live or die.

Your asking's nae sae great, lady,
   But granted it shall be ;
For ye'se won to the holy Nunnery,
   There to live or die.

But ye maun vow a vow, lady,
   Before that ye seek in ;
Never to kiss a young man's mouth,
   That goes upon the grun'.

And ye must vow anither vow,
   Severely ye must work ;
The well-warst vow that ye're to vow,
   Is never to gang to kirk.

I will vow a vow, she said,
   Before that I seek in ;
I ne'er shall kiss a young man's mouth,
   That goes upon the grun'.

And I will vow anither vow,
   Severely I will work ;
The well-warst vow that I'm to vow,
   Is never to gang to kirk.

For seven years now fair Annie,
   In the holy Nunnery lay she ;
And seven years sweet Willie lay,
   In languish like to die.

Is there nae duke nor lord's daughter,
   My son, can comfort thee ?
And save thee frae the gates o' death,
   Is there nae remedie ?

There is nae duke nor lord's daughter,
   Mother, can comfort me ;
Except it be my love, Annie,—
   In the holy Nunnery lies she.

They've dress'd sweet Willie up in silk,
   Wi' gowd his gown did shine ;
And nane cou'd ken by his pale face,
   But he was a lady fine.

So they gaed on, and farther on,
   Till they came to the yate ;
And there they spied a maiden porter,
   Wi' gowd upon her hat.

An asking, asking, maiden porter,
   An asking ye'll grant me ;
For to win in to the holy Nunnery,
   Fair Annie for to see.

Your asking's nae sae great, lady,
   But granted it shall be ;
Ye'se won into the holy Nunnery,
   Fair Annie for to see.

Be she duke's or lord's daughter,
   Its lang sin' she came here.
Fair Annie kent her true love's face,
   Says, Come up my sister dear.

Sweet Willie went to kiss her lips,
   As he had wont to do ;
But she softly whisper'd him,—
   I darena this avow.

The New Slain Knight.

My heart is lighter than the poll,
  My folly made me glad ;
As on my rambles I went out,
  Near by a garden side.

I walked on, and farther on,
  Love did my heart engage ;
There I spied a well-fair'd maid,
  Lay sleeping near a hedge.

Then I kiss'd her with my lips,
  And stroked her with my hand ;
Win up, win up, ye well-fair'd maid,
  This day ye sleep o'er lang.

This dreary sight that I hae seen,
  Unto my heart gives pain ;
At the south side o' your father's garden,
  I see a knight lies slain.

O what like was his hawk, his hawk ?
  Or what like was his hound ?
And what like was the trusty brand,
  This new-slain knight had on ?

His hawk and hound were from him gone,
  His steed tied to a tree ;
A bloody brand beneath his head,
  And on the ground lies he.

O what like was his hose, his hose ?
    And what like were his shoon ?
And what like was the gay clothing
    This new-slain knight had on ?

His coat was of the red scarlet,
    His waistcoat of the same ;
His hose were of the bonny black,
    And shoon laced with cordin.

Bonny was his yellow hair,
    For it was new comb'd down ;
Then, sighing sair, said the lady fair,
    I comb'd it late yestreen.

O wha will shoe my fair fu' foot ?
    Or wha will glove my hand ?
Or wha will father my dear bairn,
    Since my love's dead and gane ?

O I will shoe your fair fu' foot,
    And I will glove your hand ;
And I'll be father to your bairn,
    Since your love's dead and gane.

I winna father my bairn, she said,
    Upon an unkent man ;
I'll father it on the King of Heaven,
    Since my love's dead and gane.

The knight he knack'd his white fingers,
    The lady tore her hair ;
He's drawn the mask from off his face,—
    Says, Lady, mourn nae mair.

For ye are mine, and I am thine,
    I see your love is true ;
And if I live and brook my life,
    Ye'se never hae cause to rue.

The White Fisher.

It is a month, and isna mair,
    Love, sin' I was at thee ;
But find a stirring in your side,
    Who may the father be ?

Is it to a lord of might ?
    Or baron of high degree ?
Or is it to the little wee page
    That rode along wi' me ?

It is not to a man of might,
    Nor baron of high degree ;
But it is to a popish priest,
    My lord, I winna lie.

He got me in my bower alone,
    As I sat pensively ;

He vowed he would forgive my sins,
  If I would him obey.

Now it fell ance upon a day,
  This young lord went from home ;
And great and heavy were the pains,
  That came this lady on.

Then word has gane to her gude lord,
  As he sat at the wine ;
And when the tidings he did hear,
  Then he came singing hame.

When he came to his own bower door,
  He tirled at the pin ;
Ye sleep ye, wake ye, my gay lady,
  Ye'll let your gude lord in.

Huly, huly, raise she up,
  And slowly put she on,
And slowly came she to the door,—
  She was a weary woman.

Ye'll take up my son, Willie,
  That ye see here wi' me ;
And hae him down to yon shore side,
  And throw him in the sea.

Gin he sink, ye'll let him sink,
  Gin he swim, ye'll let him swim ;
And never let him return again,
  Till white fish he bring hame.

Then he's ta'en up his little young son,
   And row'd him in a band ;
And he is on to his mother,
   As fast as he could gang.

Ye'll open the door, my mother dear,
   Ye'll open, let me come in ;
My young son is in my arms twa,
   And shivering at the chin.

I tauld you true, my son Willie,
   When ye was gaun to ride,
That lady was an ill woman,
   That ye chose for your bride.

O hold your tongue, my mother dear,
   Let a' your folly be ;
I wat she is a king's daughter,
   That's sent this son to thee.

I wat she was a king's daughter,
   I lov'd beyond the sea ;
And if my lady hear of this,
   Right angry will she be.

If that be true, my son Willie,
   Your ain tongue winna lie ;
Nae waur to your son will be done,
   Than what was done to thee.

He's gane hame to his lady,
  And sair mourning was she ;
What ails you now, my lady gay,
  Ye weep sae bitterlie ?

O bonny was the white fisher,
  That I sent to the sea ;
But lang, lang, will I look for fish,
  Ere white fish he bring me !

O bonny was the white fisher,
  That ye kiest in the faem ;
But lang, lang, will I look for fish,
  Ere white fish he fetch hame !

I fell a slumbering on my bed,
  That time ye went frae me ;
And dream'd, my young son fill'd my arms,
  But when waked,—he's in the sea.

O hold your tongue, my gay lady,
  Let a' your mourning be ;
And I'll gie you some fine cordial,
  My love, to comfort thee.

I value not your fine cordial,
  Nor aught that ye can gie ;
Who could hae drown'd my bonny young son,
  Could as well poison me.

Cheer up your heart, my lily flower,
   Think nae sic ill o' me ;
Your young son's in my mother's bower,
   Set on the nourice knee.

Now if ye'll be a gude woman,
   I'll ne'er mind this to thee ;
Nae waur is done to your young son,
   That what was done to me.

Well fell's me now, my ain gude lord,
   These words do cherish me ;
If it hadna come o' yoursell, my lord,
   'Twould ne'er hae come o' me.

Lord Dingwall.

We were sisters, sisters seven,
   Bowing down, bowing down ;
The fairest women under heaven,
   And aye the birks a-bowing.

They kiest kevels them amang,
   Bowing down, bowing down ;
Wha wou'd to the grenewood gang,
   And aye the birks a-bowing.

The kevels they gied thro' the ha',
    Bowing down, bowing down ;
And on the youngest it did fa',
    And aye the birks a-bowing.

Now she must to the grenewood gang,
    Bowing down, bowing down ;
To pu' the nuts in grenewood hang,
    And aye the birks a-bowing.

She hadna tarried an hour but ane,
    Bowing down, bowing down,
Till she met wi' a highlan' groom,
    And aye the birks a bowing.

He keeped her sae late and lang,
    Bowing down, bowing down,
Till the evening set, and birds they sang,
    And aye the birks a-bowing.

He ga'e to her at their parting,
    Bowing down, bowing down,
A chain o' gold, and gay gold ring,
    And aye the birks a-bowing.

And three locks o' his yellow hair,
    Bowing down, bowing down ;
Bade her keep them for evermair,
    And aye the birks a-bowing.

When six lang months were come and gane,
   Bowing down, bowing down,
A courtier to this lady came,
   And aye the birks a-bowing.

Lord Dingwall courted this lady gay,
   Bowing down, bowing down ;
And so he set their wedding-day,
   And aye the birks a-bowing.

A little boy to the ha' was sent,
   Bowing down, bowing down ;
To bring her horse was his intent,
   And aye the birks a-bowing.

As she was riding the way along,
   Bowing down, bowing down,
She began to make a heavy moan,
   And aye the birks a-bowing.

What ails you, lady, the boy said,
   Bowing down, bowing down,
That ye seem sae dissatisfied ?
   And aye the birks a-bowing.

Are the bridle reins for you too strong ?
   Bowing down, bowing down ;
Or the stirrups for you too long ?
   And aye the birks a-bowing.

But, little boy, will ye tell me,
  Bowing down, bowing down,
The fashions that are in your countrie ?
  And aye the birks a-bowing.

The fashions in our ha' I'll tell,
  Bowing down, bowing down ;
And o' them a' I'll warn you well,
  And aye the birks a-bowing.

When ye come in upon the floor,
  Bowing down, bowing down ;
His mither will meet you wi' a golden chair,
  And aye the birks a-bowing.

But be ye maid, or be ye nane,
  Bowing down, bowing down,
Unto the high seat make ye boun',
  And aye the birks a-bowing.

Lord Dingwall aft has been beguil'd,
  Bowing down, bowing down ;
By girls whom the young men hae defiled,
  And aye the birks a-bowing.

He's cutted the paps frae their breast bane,
  Bowing down, bowing down ;
And sent them back to their ain hame,
  And aye the birks a-bowing.

When she came in upon the floor,
   Bowing down, bowing down ;
His mother met her wi' a golden chair,
   And aye the birks a-bowing.

But to the high seat she made her boun',
   Bowing down, bowing down ;
She knew that maiden she was nane,
   And aye the birks a-bowing.

When night was come they went to bed,
   Bowing down, bowing down ;
And ower her breast his arm he laid,
   And aye the birks a-bowing.

He quickly jumped upon the floor,
   Bowing down, bowing down;
And said, I've got a vile rank whore,
   And aye the birks a-bowing.

Unto his mother he made his moan,
   Bowing down, bowing down ;
Says, Mother dear, I am undone,
   And aye the birks a-bowing.

Ye've aft tald when I brought them hame,
   Bowing down, bowing down,
Whether they were maid or nane,
   And aye the birks a-bowing.

I thought I'd gotten a maiden bright,
  Bowing down, bowing down ;
I've gotten but a waefu' wight,
  And aye the birks a-bowing.

I thought I'd gotten a maiden clear,
  Bowing down, bowing down ;
But gotten but a vile rank whore,
  And aye the birks a-bowing.

When she came in upon the floor,
  Bowing down, bowing down ;
I met her wi' a golden chair,
  And aye the birks a-bowing.

But to the high seat she made her boun',
  Bowing down, bowing down ;
Because a maiden she was nane,
  And aye the birks a-bowing.

I wonder wha's tauld that gay ladie,
  Bowing bown, bowing down,
The fashion into our countrie,
  And aye the birks a-bowing.

It is your little boy I blame,
  Bowing down, bowing down;
Whom ye did send to bring her hame,
  And aye the birks a-bowing.

Then to the lady she did go,
  Bowing down, bowing down ;
And said, O Lady let me know,
  And aye the birks a-bowing.

Who has defiled your fair bodie ?
  Bowing down, bowing down ;
Ye're the first that has beguiled me,
  And aye the birks a-bowing.

O we were sisters, sisters seven,
  Bowing down, bowing down ;
The fairest women under heaven,
  And aye the birks a-bowing.

And we kiest kevels us amang,
  Bowing down, bowing down ;
Wha wou'd to the greenwood gang,
  And aye the birks a-bowing ;

For to pu' the finest flowers,
  Bowing down, bowing down ;
To put around our summer bowers,
  And aye the birks a-bowing.

I was the youngest o' them a',
  Bowing down, bowing down ;
The hardest fortune did me befa',
  And aye the birks a-bowing.

Unto the grenewood I did gang,
    Bowing down, bowing down ;
And pu'd the nuts as they down hang,
    And aye the birks a-bowing.

I hadna stay'd an hour but ane,
    Bowing down, bowing down ;
Till I met wi' a highlan' groom,
    And aye the birks a-bowing.

He keeped me sae late and lang,
    Bowing down, bowing down ;
Till the evening set, and birds they sang,
    And aye the birks a-bowing.

He gae to me at our parting,
    Bowing down, bowing down,
A chain of gold, and gay gold ring,
    And aye the birks a-bowing ;

And three locks o' his yellow hair,
    Bowing down, bowing down ;
Bade me keep them for evermair,
    And aye the birks a-bowing.

Then for to show I make nae lie,
    Bowing down, bowing down,
Look ye my trunk and ye will see,
    And aye the birks a-bowing.

Unto the trunk then she did go,
   Bowing down, bowing down,
To see if that were true or no,
   And aye the birks a-bowing.

And aye she sought, and aye she flang,
   Bowing down, bowing down,
Till these four things came to her hand,
   And aye the birks a-bowing.

Then she did to her ain son go,
   Bowing down, bowing down,
And said, my son, ye'll let me know,
   And aye the birks a-bowing.

Ye will tell to me this thing,
   Bowing down, bowing down,
What did you wi' my wedding-ring?
   And aye the birks a-bowing.

Mother dear, I'll tell nae lie,
   Bowing down, bowing down,
I gave it to a gay ladie,
   And aye the birks a-bowing.

I would gie a' my ha's and towers,
   Bowing down, bowing down,
I had this bird within my bowers,
   And aye the birks a-bowing.

Keep well, keep well, your lands and strands,
  Bowing down, bowing down ;
Ye hae that bird within your hands,
  And aye the birks a-bowing.

Now, my son, to your bower ye'll go,
  Bowing down, bowing down,
Comfort your ladie, she's full o' woe,
  And aye the birks a-bowing.

Now when nine months were come and gane,
  Bowing down, bowing down,
The lady she brought hame a son,
  And aye the birks a-bowing.

It was written on his breast bane,
  Bowing down, bowing down,
Lord Dingwall was his father's name,
  And aye the birks a-bowing.

He's ta'en his young son in his arms,
  Bowing down, bowing down,
And aye he prais'd his lovely charms,
  And aye the birks a-bowing.

And he has gi'en him kisses three,
  Bowing down, bowing down ;
And doubled them ower to his ladie,
  And aye the birks a-bowing.

James Herries.

O are ye my father, or are ye my mother?
    Or are ye my brother John?
Or are ye James Herries, my first true love,
    Come back to Scotland again?

I am not your father, I am not your mother,
    Nor am I your brother John;
But I'm James Herries, your first true love,
    Come back to Scotland again.

Awa', awa', ye former lovers,
    Had far awa' frae me;
For now I am another man's wife,
    Ye'll ne'er see joy o' me.

Had I kent that ere I came here,
    I ne'er had come to thee;
For I might hae married the king's daughter,
    Sae fain she wou'd had me.

I despised the crown o' gold,
    The yellow silk also;
And I am come to my true love,
    But with me she'll not go.

My husband he is a carpenter,
    Makes his bread on dry land,
And I hae born him a young son, —
    Wi' you I will not gang.

You must forsake your dear husband,
   Your little young son also,
Wi' me to sail the raging seas,
   Where the stormy winds do blow.

O what hae you to keep me wi',
   If I should with you go ?
If I'd forsake my dear husband,
   My little young son also ?

See ye not yon seven pretty ships,
   The eighth brought me to land ;
With merchandize and mariners,
   And wealth in every hand ?

She turn'd her round upon the shore,
   Her love's ships to behold ;
Their topmasts and their mainyards,
   Were cover'd o'er wi' gold.

Then she's gane to her little young son,
   And kiss'd him cheek and chin ;
Sae has she to her sleeping husband,
   And dune the same to him.

O sleep ye, wake ye, my husband,
   I wish ye wake in time ;
I woudna for ten thousand pounds,
   This night ye knew my mind.

She's drawn the slippers on her feet,
   Were cover'd o'er wi' gold ;
Well lined within wi' velvet fine,
   To had her frae the cold.

She hadna sailed upon the sea
   A league but barely three,
Till she minded on her dear husband,
   Her little young son tee.

O gin I were at land again,
   At land where I wou'd be,
The woman ne'er should bear the son
   Shou'd gar me sail the sea.

O hold your tongue, my sprightly flower,
   Let a' your mourning be ;
I'll show you how the lilies grow
   On the banks o' Italy.

She hadna sailed on the sea
   A day but barely ane,
Till the thoughts o' grief came in her mind,
   And she lang'd for to be hame.

O gentle death, come cut my breath,
   I may be dead ere morn ;
I may be buried in Scottish ground,
   Where I was bred and born.

O hold your tongue, my lily leesome thing,
    Let a' your mourning be ;
But for a while we'll stay at Rose Isle,
    Then see a far countrie.

Ye'se ne'er be buried in Scottish ground,
    Nor land ye'se nae mair see ;
I brought you away to punish you,
    For the breaking your vows to me.

I said ye shou'd see the lilies grow,
    On the banks o' Italy ;
But I'll let you see the fishes swim,
    In the bottom o' the sea.

He reach'd his hand to the topmast,
    Made a' the sails gae down ;
And in the twinkling o' an e'e,
    Baith ship and crew did drown.

The fatal flight o' this wretched maid
    Did reach her ain countrie ;
Her husband then distracted ran,
    And this lament made he :—

O wae be to the ship, the ship,
    And wae be to the sea,
And wae be to the mariners,
    Took Jeanie Douglas frae me !

O bonny, bonny was my love,
  A pleasure to behold ;
The very hair o' my love's head,
  Was like the threads o' gold.

O bonny was her cheek, her cheek,
  And bonny was her chin ;
And bonny was the bride she was,
  The day she was made mine !

Barbara Blair.

Barbara Blair came down the stair,
  A gown o' green she did put on ;
Wi' siller slippers on her feet,—
  The captain's made her colour wan.

The captain's on to yon harbour,
  To rig his bonny ship for sea ;
O daintie Babie, said her mother,
  Tho' he shou'd ne'er come back to thee.

I wish Saturday was a stormy day,
  A mighty tempest in the sea ;
The captain's ship may rent and rive,
  And he may ne'er come back to thee.

O say not sae, my mother dear,
  He laid the red gowd on my knee ;
Now daintie Babie, said her mother,
  This same red gowd will marry thee.

If I wou'd marry a lord o' fame,
   He is abeen my ain degree ;
For aye when I offended him,
   He wou'd cast up my babe to me.

I wish Saturday was a bonny day,
   A mighty calmness in the sea ;
That ships may sail, and boats may row,
   That my dear captain come back to me.

But I will cut my yellow hair,
   I'll cut it fair abeen my e'e ;
And I will on to yonder harbour,
   See gin the captain will mind me.

The captain heard his true love's voice,
   And he did stand below the stair ;
And into Babie's room he went,
   Said, Love, let be your yellow hair.

He's ta'en out three handfu' o' gowd,
   And he has tauld it on his knee ;
Then he raxed ower the table braid,
   And said, My love take this frae me.

He put his hand into his pocket,
   And he's ta'en out a bottle o' wine ;
Bring me a cup, mother, he says,
   Ere I drink Babie's health and mine.

Brawlin' gaed the auld wife but,
　And brawlin' came the auld wife ben ;
And put the cup into his hand,
　She wish'd it might be rank poison.

He's ta'en the cup into his hand,
　Into the cup he pour'd the wine ;
Here is your health, mother, he said,
　I'm sure ye wish your son the same.

He's put his hand in his pocket,
　And he's ta'en out the marriage lines ;
And put them in the auld wife's hand,
　Said, Mother, can ye read the same ?

Now when she look'd these lines upon,
　I wyte a light laugh then gae she ;
O wae betide ye, captain, she said,
　Ye're aye sae fu' o' policy !

O, mother, now gae make a bed,
　And ye will make it saft and fine ;
And lay my Babie at my side,
　The place she shou'd lien in langsyne.

Her mother she did make a bed,
　And she has made it saft and fine ;
And laid his Babie at his side,
　The place she shou'd lien in langsyne.

Barefoot ga'ed the auld wife but,
　　And barefoot came the auld wife ben ;
For fear o' waking the captain,
　　And's bonny Babie lien beyon'.

Thomas o' Yonderdale.

Lady Maisry lives intill a bower,
　　She never wore but what she would ;
Her gowns were o' the silks sae fine,
　　Her coats stood up wi' bolts o' gold.

'Mony a knight there courted her,
　　And gentlemen o' high degree ;
But it was Thomas o' Yonderdale,
　　That gain'd the love o' this ladie.

Now he has hunted her till her bower,
　　Baith late at night, and the mid day ;
But when he stole her virgin rose,
　　Nae mair this maid he would come nigh.

But it fell ance upon a time,
　　Thomas, her bower he walked by ;
There he saw her, Lady Maisry,
　　Nursing her young son on her knee.

O seal on you, my bonny babe,
　　And lang may ye my comfort be ;
Your father passes by our bower,
　　And now minds neither you nor me.

Now when Thomas heard her speak,
   The saut tear trinkled frae his e'e ;
To Lady Maisry's bower he went,
   Says, Now I'm come to comfort thee.

Is this the promise ye did make,
   Last when I was in your companie ?
You said before nine months were gane,
   Your wedded wife that I should be.

If Saturday be a bonny day,
   Then, my love, I maun sail the sea ;
But if I live for to return,
   O then, my love, I'll marry thee.

I wish Saturday a stormy day,
   High and stormy be the sea ;
Ships may not sail, nor boats row,
   But gar true Thomas stay wi' me.

Saturday was a bonny day,
   Fair and leesome blew the wind ;
Ships did sail, and boats did row,
   Which had true Thomas to unco ground.

He hadna been on unco ground,
   A month, a month, but scarcely three,
Till he has courted another maid,
   And quite forgotten Lady Maisry.

Ae night as he lay on his bed,
  In a dreary dream dreamed he,
That Maisry stood by his bedside,
  Upbraiding him for's inconstancie.

He's call'd upon his little boy,
  Says, bring me candle, that I see ;
And ye maun gang this night, boy,
  Wi' a letter to a gay ladie.

It is my duty you to serve,
  And bring you coal and candle light,
And I would rin your errand, master,
  If 'twere to Lady Maisry bright.

Tho' my legs were sair I cou'dna gang,
  Tho' the night were dark I cou'dna see,
Tho' I should creep on hands and feet,
  I wou'd gae to Lady Maisry.

Win up, win up, my bonny boy,
  And at my bidding for to be ;
For ye maun quickly my errand rin,
  For it is to Lady Maisry.

Ye'll bid her dress in the gowns o' silk,
  Likewise in the coats o' cramasie ;
Ye'll bid her come alang wi' you,
  True Thomas's wedding for to see.

Ye'll bid her shoe her steed before,
   And a' gowd graithing him behind ;
On ilka tip o' her horse mane,
   Twa bonny bells to loudly ring.

And on the tor o' her saddle,
   A courtly bird to sweetly sing ;
Her bridle reins o' silver fine,
   And stirrups by her side to hing.

She dress'd her in the finest silk,
   Her coats were o' the cramasie ;
And she's awa' to unco land,
   True Thomas's wedding for to see.

At ilka tippet o' her horse mane,
   Twa bonny bells did loudly ring ;
And on the tor o' her saddle,
   A courtly bird did sweetly sing.

The bells they rang, the bird he sang,
   As they rode in yon pleasant plain ;
Then soon she met true Thomas's bride
   Wi' a' her maidens and young men.

The bride she garned round about,
   I wonder, said she, who this may be ?
It surely is our Scottish Queen,
   Come here our wedding for to see.

Out it speaks true Thomas's boy,
   She maunna lift her head sae hie;
But it's true Thomas's first love,
   Come here your wedding for to see.

Then out bespake true Thomas's bride,
   I wyte the tear did blind her e'e;
If this be Thomas's first true love,
   I'm sair afraid he'll ne'er hae me.

Then in it came her Lady Maisry,
   And aye as she trips in the fleer;
What is your will, Thomas, she said,
   This day, ye know, ye call'd me here?

Come hither by me, ye lily flower,
   Come hither, and set ye down by me;
For ye're the ane I've call'd upon,
   And ye my wedded wife maun be.

Then in it came true Thomas's bride,
   And aye as she tripp'd on the stane;
What is your will, Thomas, she said,
   This day, ye know, ye call'd me hame?

Ye hae come on hired horseback,
   But ye'se gae hame in coach sae free;
For here's the flower into my bower,
   I mean my wedded wife shall be.

O ye will break your lands, Thomas,
  And part them in divisions three ;
Gie twa o' them to your ae brother,
  And cause your brother marry me.

I winna break my lands, he said,
  For ony woman that I see ;
My brother's a knight o' wealth and might,
  He'll wed naue but he will for me.

The Knight's Ghost.

There is a fashion in this land,
  And even come to this country ;
That every lady should meet her lord,
  When he is newly come frae sea.

Some wi' hawks and some wi' hounds,
  And other some wi' gay monie ;
But I will gae myself alone,
  And set his young son on his knee.

She's ta'en her young son in her arms,
  And nimbly walk'd by yon sea strand ;
And there she spy'd her father's ship,
  As she was sailing to dry land.

Where hae ye put my ain gude lord,
  This day he stays sae far frae me ?
If ye be wanting your ain gude lord,
  A sight o' him ye'll never see.

Was he brunt, or was he shot?
   Or was he drowned in the sea?
Or what's become o' my ain gude lord,
   That he will ne'er appear to me?

He wasna brunt, nor was he shot,
   Nor was he drowned in the sea ;
He was slain in Dunfermling,
   A fatal day to you and me.

Come in, come in, my merry young men,
   Come in and drink the wine wi' me ;
And a' the better ye shall fare,
   For this gude news ye tell to me.

She's brought them down to yon cellar,
   She brought them fifty steps and three ;
She birled wi' them the beer and wine,
   Till they were as drunk as drunk could be.

Then she has lock'd her cellar door,
   For there were fifty steps and three ;
Lie there wi' my sad malison,
   For this bad news ye've tauld to me.

She's ta'en the keys intill her hand,
   And threw them deep, deep in the sea ;
Lie there wi' my sad malison,
   Till my gude lord return to me.

Then she sat down in her own room,
   And sorrow lull'd her fast asleep ;
And up it starts her own gude lord,
   And even at that lady's feet.

Take here the keys, Janet, he says,
   That ye threw deep, deep in the sea ;
And ye'll relieve my merry young men,
   For they've nane o' the swick* o' me,

They shot the shot, and drew the stroke,
   And wad in red bluid to the knee ;
Nae sailors mair for their lord cou'd do,
   Nor my young men they did for me.

I hae a question at you to ask,
   Before that ye depart frae me ;
You'll tell to me what day I'll die,
   And what day will my burial be ?

I hae nae mair o' God's power
   Than he has granted unto me ;
But come to heaven when ye will,
   There porter to you I will be.

But ye'll be wed to a finer knight
   Than ever was in my degree ;
Unto him ye'll hae children nine,
   And six o' them will be ladies free.

* Swick, blame.

The other three will be bold young men.
 To fight for king and countrie ;
The ane a duke, the second a knight,
 And third a laird o' lands sae free.

The Trooper and Fair Maid.

One evening as a maid did walk,
 The moon was shining clearly ;
She heard a trooper at the gates,
 She thought it was her dearie.
She's ta'en his horse then by the head,
 And led him to the stable ;
And gi'en to him baith corn and hay,
 To eat what he was able.
Chorus.—Bonny lass, gin I come near you,
  Bonny lass, gin I come near you ;
  I'll gar a' your ribbons reel,
   Bonny lass, or e'er I lea' you.

She's ta'en the trooper by the hand,
 And led him to the table ;
And furnish'd him wi' bread and cheese,
 To eat what he was able.
She's ta'en the wine glass in her hand,
 Poured out the wine sae clearly ;
Here is your health and mine, she cried,
 And ye're welcome hame, my deary !
  Bonny lass, &c.

A glass o' wine for gentlemen,
   And bonny lads for lasses ;
And bread and cheese for cavaliers,
   And corn and hay for asses.
Then she went but and made his bed,
   She made it like a lady ;
And she coost aff her mankie gown,
   Says, Laddie, are you ready ?
      Bonny lass, &c.

Then he coost aff his big watch coat,
   But and his silken beaver ;
A pair o' pistols frae his side,
   And he lay down beside her.
Bonny lassie, I am wi' you now,
   Bonny lassie, I am wi' you ;
But I'll gar a' your ribbons reel,
   Bonny lassie, ere I lea' you.

The trumpet sounds thro' Birldale,
   Says, Men and horse, make ready ;
The drums do beat at Staneman hill,—
   Lads, leave your mam and daddie.
The fifes did play at Cromley banks,
   Lads, Leave the Lewas o' Fyvie ;
And then the trooper he got up,
   Says, Lassie, I must lea' you now.

Bonny lassie, I maun lea' you now,
   Bonny lassie, I maun lea' you ;
But if ever I come this road again,
   I will come in and see you.

She's ta'en her gown out ower her arms,
   And followed him to Stirling;
And aye the trooper he did say,
   O turn ye back, my darling.
O when will we twa meet again ?
   Or when will you me marry ?
When rashin rinds grow gay gowd rings,
   I winna langer tarry.
      Bonny lassie, &c.

O when will we twa meet again ?
   Or when will you me marry ?
When heather knaps grow siller taps,
   I winna langer tarry.
O when will we twa meet again ?
   Or when will you me marry ?
When heather cows grow owsen bows,
   I winna langer tarry.
      Bonny lassie, &c.

O when will we twa meet again ?
   Or when will you me marry ?
When cockle shells grow siller bells,
   I winna langer tarry.
O when will we twa meet again ?
   Or when will you me marry ?
When apple trees grow in the seas,
   I winna langer tarry.
      Bonny lass, &c.

O when will we twa meet again ?
   Or when will you me marry ?

When fishes fly, and seas gang dry,
  I winna langer tarry.
O when will we twa meet again ?
  Or when will you me marry ?
When frost and snaw shall warm us a',
  I winna langer tarry.
        Bonny lassie, &c.

Yestreen I was my daddie's dow,
  But an' my mamy's dawtie ;
This night I gang wi' bairn to you,
  Waes me that I e'er saw thee !
Yestreen ye were your daddie's dow,
  But an' your mammie's dawtie ;
But gin ye gang wi' bairn to me,
  Ye may rue that e'er ye saw me.
        Bonny lassie, &c.

O turn back, my bonny lass,
  O turn back, my dearie ;
For the Highland hills are ill to climb,
  And the bluidy swords wou'd fear ye.
        Bonny lassie, &c.

Lord Ingram and Childe Vyet.

Lord Ingram and Childe Vyet
  Were baith born in ae bower ;
They fell in love wi' ae lady,
  Their honour was but poor.

Lord Ingram and Childe Vyet
   Were baith bred in ae ha';
They laid their love on Lady Maisry,
   The waur did them befa'.

Lord Ingram gained Lady Maisry
   Frae father and frae mother;
Lord Ingram gained Lady Maisry
   Frae sister and frae brother.

Lord Ingram gained Lady Maisry
   Frae a' her kith and kin;
Lord Ingram courted Lady Maisry,
   But she said nay to him.

Lord Ingram courted Lady Maisry,
   In the garden amo' the flowers;
Childe Vyet courted Lady Maisry
   Amo' her ha's and bowers.

Lord Ingram sent to Lady Maisry,
   A steed, paced fu' well;
She wishes he were ower the sea,
   If Childe Vyet were well.

Lord Ingram courted Lady Maisry
   Frae her relations a';
Childe Vyet courted Lady Maisry
   Amo' the sheets sae sma'.

Lord Ingram bought to Lady Maisry
  The siller knapped gloves ;
She wish'd his hands might swell in them,
  Had she her ain true love.

Lord Ingram bought to Lady Maisry
  The brands garnish'd wi' steel ;
She wish'd the same might pierce his heart,
  Gin Childe Vyet were weell.

Childe Vyet bought to Lady Maisry
  The fancy ribbons sma' ;
She had mair delight in her sma' fancy
  Than o' Lord Ingram, gowd and a'.

Lord Ingram's gane to her father,
  And thus he did complain ;—
O, am I doom'd, to die for love,
  And nae be loved again ?

I hae sent to your daughter
  The steed paced fu' well ;
She wishes I were ower the sea,
  Gin Childe Vyet were well.

I hae bought to your daughter
  The siller knapped gloves ;
She wish'd my hands might swell in them,
  Had she her ain true love.

I hae bought to your daughter
   The brands garnish'd wi' steel;
She wish'd the same might pierce my heart,
   Gin Childe Vyet were weell.

Childe Vyet bought to your daughter
   The fancy ribbons sma';
She's mair delight in her sma' fancy,
   Nor o' me, gowd and a'.

Her father turn'd him round about,
   A solemn oath sware he;
Saying, She shall be the bride this night,
   And you bridegroom shall be.

O had your tongue, my father dear,
   Let a' your passion be;
The reason that I love this man,
   It is unknown to thee.

Sweetly played the merry organs,
   Intill her mother's bower;
But still and dum stood Lady Maisry,
   And let the tears down pour.

Sweetly played the harp sae fine,
   Intill her father's ha';
But still and dum stood Lady Maisry,
   And let the tears down fa'.

'Tween Marykirk and her mother's bower,
  Was a' clad ower wi' gowd ;
For keeping o' her snaw-white feet
  Frae treading o' the mould.

Lord Ingram gaed in at ae church-door,
  Childe Vyet at another ;
And lightly leugh him, Childe Vyet,
  At Lord Ingram, his brother.

O laugh ye at my men, brother ?
  Or do ye laugh at me ?
Or laugh ye at young Lady Maisry,
  This night my bride's to be ?

I laugh na at your men, brother,
  Nor do I laugh at thee ;
But I laugh at the knightless sport
  That I saw wi' my e'e.

It is a ring on ae finger,
  A broach on ae breast bane ;
And if ye kent what's under that,
  Your love wou'd soon be dane.

Lord Ingram and his merry young men
  Out ower the plains are gane :
And pensively walk'd him, Childe Vyet,
  Him single, self, alane.

When they had eaten and well drunken,
  And a' men bound for bed ;
Lord Ingram and Lady Maisry,
  In ae chamber were laid.

He laid his hand upon her breast,
  And thus pronounced he :—
There is a bairn within your sides,
  Wha may the father be ?

Wha ever be your bairn's father,
  Ye will father it on me ;
The fairest castle o' Snowdon
  Your morning gift shall be.

Wha ever be my bairn's father,
  I'll ne'er father it on thee ;
For better love I my bairn's father
  Nor ever I'll love thee.

Then he's taen out a trusty brand,
  Laid it between them tway ;
Says, Lye ye there, ye ill woman,
  A maid for me till day.

Next morning her father came,
  Well belted, and a brand ;
Then up it starts him, Lord Ingram,
  He was an angry man.

If your daughter had been a gude woman,
   As I thought she had been,
Cauld iron shou'd hae never lien
   The lang night us between.

Ohon, alas! my daughter dear,
   What's this I hear o' thee?
I thought ye was a gude woman
   As in the north countrie!

O had your tongue, my father dear,
   Let a' your sorrows be;
I never liked Lord Ingram,—
   Ye ken ye forced me.

Then in it came him Chylde Vyet,
   Well belted, and a brand;
Then up it raise him Lord Ingram,—
   He was an angry man.

Win up, win up, now Lord Ingram,
   Rise up immediately;
That you and I the quarrel try,
   Who gains the victory.

I hae twa brands in ae scabbard,
   That cost me mony pound;
Take ye the best, gie me the warst,
   And I'll fight where I stand.

Then up it starts him Childe Vyet
  Shook back his yellow hair ;
The first an' stroke Childe Vyet drew,
  He wounded Ingram sair.

Then up it starts him Lord Ingram,
  Shed back his coal-black hair ;
The first an' stroke Lord Ingram drew,
  Childe Vyet needed nae mair.

Nae meen was made for these twa knights,
  Whan they were lying dead ;
But a' for her, Lady Maisry.
  That gaes in mournfu' weed.

Says, If I hae been an ill woman,
  Alas ! and wae is me ;
And if I've been an ill woman,
  A gude woman I'll be !

Ye'll take frae me my silk attire,
  Bring me a palmer's weed ;
And through the warld, for their sakes,
  I'll gang and beg my bread.

If I gang a step for Childe Vyet,
  For Lord Ingram I'll gang three ;
All for the honour that he paid
  At Marykirk to me.

I'll gang a step for Child Vyet,
  For Lord Ingram I'll gang three;
It was into my mother's bower
  Childe Vyet wronged me!

Castle Ha's Daughter.

As Annie sat into her bower,
  A thought came in her head,
That she would gang to gude greenwood,
  Across the flowery mead.

She hadna pu'd a flower, a flower,
  Nor broken a branch but twa;
Till by it came a gentle squire,
  Says, Lady come awa'.

There's nane that comes to gude greenwood
  But pays to me a tein;
And I maun hae your maidenhead,
  Or than your mantle green.

My mantle's o' the finest silk,
  Anither I can spin;
But gin you take my maidenhead,
  The like I'll never fin'.

He ta'en her by the milk-white hand,
  And by the grass-green sleeve,
There laid her low in gude greenwood,
  And at her spier'd nae leave.

When he had got his wills o' her,
 His wills as he had ta'en ;
She said, if you rightly knew my birth,
 Ye'd better letten alane.

Is your father a lord o' might ?
 Or baron o' high degree ?
Or what race are ye sprung frae,
 That I should lat ye be ?

O, I am Castle Ha's daughter,
 O' birth and high degree ;
And if he knows what ye hae done,
 He'll hang you on a tree.

If ye be Castle Ha's daughter,
 This day I am undone ;
If ye be Castle Ha's daughter,
 I am his only son.

Ye lie, ye lie, ye jelly hind squire,
 Sae loud as I hear yon lie ;
Castle Ha', he has but ae dear son,
 And he is far beyond the sea.

O I am Castle Ha's dear son,
 A word I dinna lie ;
Yes ! I am Castle Ha's dear son,
 And new come o'er the sea.

'Twas yesterday, that fatal day,
　　That I did cross the faem ;
I wish my bonny ship had sunk,
　　And I had ne'er come hame.

Then dowie, dowie, raise she up,
　　And dowie came she hame,
And stripped aff her silk mantle,
　　And then to bed she's gane.

Then in it came her mother dear,
　　And she steps in the fleer ;
Win up, win up, now fair Annie,
　　What makes your lying here ?

This morning fair as I went out,
　　Near by yon castle wa',
Great and heavy was the stane
　　That on my foot did fa'.

Hae I nae ha's, hae I nae bowers ?
　　Towers, or mony a town ?
Will not these cure your bonny foot,
　　Gar you gae hale and soun' ?

Ye hae ha's, and ye hae bowers,
　　And towers, and mony a town ;
But nought will cure my bonny foot,
　　Gar me gang hale and soun'.

Then in it came her father dear,
    And he trips in the fleer;
Win up, win up, now fair Annie,
    What makes your lying here?

This morning fair, as I went out,
    Near by yon castle wa',
Great and heavy was the stane
    That on my foot did fa'.

Hae I nae ha's, hae I nae bowers,
    And towers, and mony a town?
Will not these cure your bonny foot,
    Gar you gang hale and soun'?

O, ye hae ha's, and ye hae bowers,
    And towers, and mony a town;
But nought will cure my bonny foot,
    Gar me gang hale and soun'.

Then in it came her sister Grace,
    As she steps in the fleer;
Win up, win up, now fair Annie,
    What makes your lying here?

Win up, and see your ae brother,
    That's new come ower the sea;
Ohon, alas! says fair Annie,
    He spake ower soon wi' me.

To her room her brother's gane,
  Stroked back her yellow hair;
To her lips his ain did press,
  But words spake never mair.

Willie's Drowned in Gamery.

O Willie is fair, and Willie is rare,
  And Willie is wond'rous bonny;
And Willie says he'll marry me,
  Gin ever he marry ony.

O, ye'se get James, or ye'se get George,
  Or ye'se get bonny Johnnie;
Ye'se get the flower o' a' my sons,
  Gin ye'll forsake my Willie.

O, what care I for James or George,
  Or yet for bonny Peter?
I dinna value their love a leek,
  An' I getna Willie the writer.

O, Willie has a bonny hand,
  And dear but it is bonny;
He has nae mair for a' his land,
  What wou'd ye do wi' Willie?

O, Willie has a bonny face,
   And dear but it is bonny :
But Willie has nae other grace,
   What wou'd ye do wi' Willie ?

Willie's fair, and Willie's rare,
   And Willie's wond'rous bonny ;
There's nane wi' him that can compare,
   I love him best of ony.

On Wednesday, that fatal day,
   The people were convening ;
Besides all this, threescore and ten,
   To gang to the bridesteel wi' him.

Ride on, ride on, my merry men a',
   I've forgot something behind me ;
I've forgot to get my mother's blessing,
   To gae to the bridesteel wi' me.

Your Peggy she's but bare fifteen,
   And ye are scarcely twenty ;
The water o' Gamery is wide and braid,
   My heavy curse gang wi' thee !

Then they rode on, and further on,
   Till they came on to Gamery ;
The wind was loud, the stream was proud,
   And wi' the stream gaed Willie.

Then they rode on, and further on,
    Till they came to the kirk o' Gamery;
And every one on high horse sat,
    But Willie's horse rade toomly.

When they were settled at that place,
    The people fell a mourning;
And a council held amo' them a',
    But sair, sair wept Kinmundy,

Then out it speaks the bride hersell,
    Says, What means a' this mourning?
Where is the man amo' them a',
    That shou'd gie me fair wedding?

Then out it speaks his brother John,
    Says, Meg, I'll tell you plainly,
The stream was strong, the clerk rade wrong,
    And Willie's drown'd in Gamery.

She put her hand up to her head,
    Where were the ribbons many;
She rave them a', let them down fa',
    And straightway ran to Gamery.

She sought it up, she sought it down,
    Till she was wet and weary;
And in the middle part o' it,
    There she got her deary.

Then she stroak'd back his yellow hair,
   And kiss'd his mou' sae comely ;
My mother's heart's be as wae as thine,
   We'se baith sleep in the water o' Gamery.

Lang Johnny Moir.

There lives a man in Rynie's land,
   Anither in Auchindore ;
The bravest lad amo' them a',
   Was lang Johnny Moir.

Young Johnny was an airy blade,
   Fu' sturdy, stout, and strang ;
The sword that hang by Johnny's side,
   Was just full ten feet lang.

Young Johnny was a clever youth,
   Fu' sturdy, stout, and wight ;
Just full three yards around the waist,
   And fourteen feet in hight.

But if a' be true they tell me now,
   And a' be true I hear ;
Young Johnny's on to Lundan gane,
   The king's banner to bear.

He hadna been in fair Lundan
   But twalmonths twa or three,
Till the fairest lady in a' Lundan
   Fell in love wi' young Johnny.

This news did sound thro' Lundan town,
 Till it came to the king,
That the muckle Scot had fa'in in love
 Wi' his daughter, Lady Jean.

When the king got word o' that,
 A solemn oath sware he ;
This weighty Scot sall strait a rope,
 And hanged he shall be.

When Johnny heard the sentence past,
 A light laugh then gae he ;
While I hae strength to wield my blade,
 Ye darena a' hang me.

The English dogs were cunning rogues,
 About him they did creep,
And ga'e him drops o' lodomy
 That laid him fast asleep.

Whan Johnny waken'd frae his sleep,
 A sorry heart had he ;
His jaws and hands in iron bands,
 His feet in fetters three.

O whar will I get a little wee boy
 Will work for meat and fee ;
That will rin on to my uncle,
 At the foot of Benachie ?

Here am I, a little wee boy,
    Will work for meat and fee;
That will rin on to your uncle,
    At the foot of Benachie.

Whan ye come whar grass grows green,
    Slack your shoes and rin;
And whan ye come whar water's strong,
    Ye'll bend your bow and swim.

And whan ye come to Benachie,
    Ye'll neither chap nor ca';
Sae well's ye'll ken auld Johnny there,
    Three feet abeen them a'.

Ye'll gie to him this braid letter,
    Seal'd wi' my faith and troth;
And ye'll bid him bring alang wi' him
    The body, Jock o' Noth.

Whan he came whar grass grew green,
    He slack't his shoes and ran;
And whan he came whar water's strong,
    He bent his bow and swam.

And whan he came to Benachie,
    Did neither chap nor ca';
Sae well's he kent auld Johnny there,
    Three feet abeen them a'.

What news, what news, my little wee boy ?
    Ye never were here before ;
Nae news, nae news, but a letter from
    Your nephew, Johnny Moir.

Ye'll take here this braid letter,
    Seal'd wi' his faith and troth ;
And ye're bidden bring alang wi' you,
    The body, Jock o' Noth.

Benachie lyes very low,
    The tap o' Noth lyes high ;
For a' the distance that's between,
    He heard auld Johnny cry.

Whan on the plain these champions met,
    Twa grizly ghosts to see ;
There were three feet between their brows,
    And shoulders were yards three.

These men they ran ower hills and dales,
    And ower mountains high ;
Till they came on to Lundan town,
    At the dawn o' the third day.

And whan they came to Lundan town,
    The yetts were lockit wi' bands ;
And wha were there but a trumpeter,
    Wi' trumpet in his hands.

What is the matter, ye keepers all ;
    Or what's the matter within,
That the drums do beat, and bells do ring,
    And make sic dolefu' din ?

There's naething the matter, the keeper said,
    There's naething the matter to thee ;
But a weighty Scot to strait the rope,
    And the morn he maun die.

O open the yetts, ye proud keepers,
    Ye'll open without delay ;
The trembling keeper, smiling, said,—
    O I hae not the key.

Ye'll open the yetts, ye proud keepers,
    Ye'll open without delay ;
Or here is a body at my back,
    Frae Scotland hae brought the key.

Ye'll open the yetts, says Jock o' Noth,
    Ye'll open them at my call ;
Then wi' his foot he has drove in
    Three yards braid o' the wall.

As they gaed in by Drury-lane,
    And down by the town's hall ;
And there they saw young Johnny Moir,
    Stand on their English wall.

Ye're welcome here, my uncle dear,
 Ye're welcome unto me;
Ye'll loose the knot, and slack the rope,
 And set me frae the tree.

Is it for murder, or for theft ?
 Or is it for robberie ?
If it is for ony heinous crime,
 There's nae remeid for thee.

It's nae for murder, nor for theft,
 Nor yet for robberie ;
A' is for the loving a gay lady,
 They're gaun to gar me die.

O whar's thy sword, says Jock o' Noth,
 Ye brought frae Scotland wi' thee ?
I never saw a Scotsman yet,
 But cou'd wield a sword or tree.

A pox upo' their lodomy,
 On me had sic a sway ;
Four o' their men, the bravest four,
 They bore my blade away.

Bring back his blade, says Jock o' Noth,
 And freely to him it gie ;
Or I hae sworn a black Scot's oath,
 I'll gar five million die.

Now whar's the lady, says Jock o' Noth,
   Sae fain I wou'd her see ?
She's lock'd up in her ain chamber,
   The king he keeps the key.

So they hae gane before the king,
   With courage bauld and free ;
Their armour bright cast sic a light,
   That almost dim'd his e'e.

O whar's the lady, says Jock o' Noth,
   Sae fain as I wou'd her see ?
For we are come to her wedding,
   Frae the foot o' Benachie.

O take the lady, said the king,
   Ye welcome are for me ;
I never thought to see sic men
   Frae the foot o' Benachie.

If I had ken'd, said Jock o' Noth,
   Ye'd wonder'd sae muckle at me,
I wou'd hae brought ane larger far
   By sizes three times three.

Likewise if I had thought I'd been
   Sic a great fright to thee,
I'd brought Sir John o' Erskine park,
   He's thretty feet and three.

Wae to the little boy, said the king,
   Brought tidings unto thee ;
Let all England say what they will,
   High hanged shall he be.

O if ye hang the little wee boy
   Brought tidings unto me ;
We shall attend his burial,
   And rewarded ye shall be.

O take the lady, said the king,
   And the boy shall be free :
A priest, a priest, then Johnny cried,
   To join my love and me.

A clerk, a clerk, the king replied,
   To seal her tocher wi' thee.
Out it speaks auld Johnny then,
   These words pronounced he :—

I wantnae lands and rents at hame,
   I'll ask nae gowd frae thee ;
I am possess'd o' riches great,
   Hae fifty ploughs and three ;
Likewise fa's heir to ane estate
   At the foot o' Benachie.

Hae ye ony masons in this place,
   Or ony at your call,
That ye may now send some o' them,
   To build your broken wall ?

Yes, there are masons in this place,
    And plenty at my call ;
But ye may gang frae whence ye came,
    Never mind my broken wall.

They've ta'en the lady by the hand,
    And set her prison free ;
Wi' drums beating, and fifes playing,
    They spent the night wi' glee.

Now, auld Johnny Moir, and young Johnny
        Moir,
    And Jock o' Noth, a' three,
The English lady, and little wee boy,
    Went a' to Benachie !

Cuttie's Wedding.

Busk and go, busk and go,
    Busk and go to Cuttie's wedding ;
Wha wou'd be the lass or lad
    That wudna gang, an' they waur biddin ?

Cuttie, he's a lang man,
    O, he'll get a little wifie ;
But he'll tak' on to the town loan,
    Fan she takes on her fickie fickie.
            Busk and go, &c.

Cuttie he came here yestreen,
    Cuttie he fell ower the midden ;
He wat his hose, and tint his sheen,
    Courting at a canker'd maiden.
        Busk and go, &c.

He set him down upo' the green,
    The lass cam' till him wi' ae bidden ;
He says, Gin ye war mine, my dame,
    Mony ane's be at our wedding.

Busk and go, busk and go,
    Busk and go to Cuttie's wedding ;
Wha wou'd be the lass or lad
    That wudna gang, an' they waur biddin?

Miss Gordon of Gight.

O whare are ye gaeing, bonny Miss Gordon ?
    O whare are ye gaeing, sae bonny and braw ?
Ye've married wi' Johnny Byron,
    To squander the lands o' Gight awa'.

This youth is a rake, frae England is come,
    The Scots dinna ken his extraction ava ;
He keeps up his misses, his landlords he duns,
    That's fast drawn the lands o' Gight awa'.
        O whare are ye gaeing, &c.

The shooting o' guns, and rattling o' drums,
  The bugle in woods, the pipes in the ha';
The beagles a howling, the hounds a growling,
  These soundings will soon gar Gight gang awa'.
    O whare are ye gaeing, &c.

The Man to the Green Joe.

Early in the morning, the cat she crew day,
  Quo' the man to the joe, quo' the man to the joe;
The cock saddled's steed, and fast he rade away,
  Quo' the merry, merry man to the green, joe.

He saddled the spur, and he bridled the mane,
  Quo' the man to the joe, quo' the man to the joe;
And he rade on the rumple, wi' the tail in his hand,
  Quo' the merry, merry man to the green, joe.

As he rade by the mill, the mass it was singing,
  Quo' the man to the joe, quo' the man to the joe;
When he came by the kirk, the corn it was grinding,
  Quo' the merry, merry man to the green, joe.

The gudeman o' the mill, they cau'd him Gibbie Reid,
  Quo' the man to the joe, quo' the man to the joe;
Wi' his bonnet on his feet, and his breeks on his
    head,
  Quo' the merry, merry man to the green, joe.

Forth came the maiden, the auld millar's mither,
  Quo' the man to the joe, quo' the man to the joe ;
Riddling at her green cheese and winnowing at her
    butter,
  Quo' the merry, merry man to the green, joe.

There were fowr an' twenty headless men playing at
    the ba',
  Quo' the man to the joe, quo' the man to the joe ;
But by came footless, and took her frae them a',
  Quo' the merry, merry man to the green, joe.

Up starts Mouless, and merrily he leuch,
  Quo' the man to the joe, quo' the man to the joe ;
And upstarts Tongueless, and tauld's tale teuch,
  Quo' the merry, merry man to the green, joe.

Four an' twenty Hilandmen chasing at a snail,
  Quo' the man to the joe, quo' the man to the joe ;
O, says the hindmast, weel take her by the tail,
  Quo' the merry, merry man to the green, joe.

The snail set up her horns like ony humle cow,
  Quo' the man to the joe, quo' the man to the joe ;
Fye, says the foremost, we're a' sticket now,
  Quo' the merry, merry man to the green, joe.

Ower Benachie I saw a skate flee,
  Quo' the man to the joe, quo' the man to the joe ;
And four an' twenty little anes fleeing her wi',
  Quo' the merry, merry man to the green, joe.

Four an' twenty skate's birds in a drake's nest,
　Quo' the man to the joe, quo' the man to the joe ;
And they turn'd them about wi' their heads to the
　　west,
　Quo' the merry, merry man to the green, joe.

Auld Scour Abeen.

Scour abeen, bonny lass,
　And dinna wrang my pan ;
The puddings now they maun be made,
　Wi' a' the haste ye can.
The day I hae a gude fat cow,
　That's to be kill'd right seen ;
We's hae a hearty Christmas,
　Said auld Scour Abeen.

'Tis for the puddings o' my cow,
　As I may live and die,
I will declare upo' my word,
　I scarcely had but three.
My housekeeper and a' her bairns,
　They ate them ane by ane ;
O seven podducks in her wyme,
　And ane, quo' Scour Abeen.

Whan the puds war sodden,
　And weel hung up to dry,
Our little couzin Jockie, there,
　Took down a pud to try ;
But O it had been telling him,
　That he had been in Rome ;
For when he saw the black belt,
　Well kent he then his doom.

The Wee Bridalie.

There was a little wee bridal,
　A bridal in Auchendown ;
And there was but a little gude meat,
　And as few folk did come.
A black sheep's head in the pot,
　A sheep's head wanting the tongue ;
And O, said the silly bridegroom,
　Our meat will soon be done.

A wee sup ale in an anker,
　A wee sup ale in a tun ;
And O, said the silly bridegroom,
　I pray you leave me some.

VOL. I.　　　　　S

When they had eaten and drunken,
  The pipes began to bum ;
And O, said the silly bridegroom,
  I kent this day wou'd cum.

When they were serv'd wi' mirth,
  The bride to bed was boon ;
And O, said the silly bridegroom,
  There's nane see me ly down ;

There's nane see me ly down,
  Amo' the sheets sae sma' ;
The bride she's ly at the bed-stock,
  And I'll ly niest the wa'.

The Little Man.

As I gaed out to tak' the air,
  Between Midmar and bonny Craigha' ;
There I met a little wee man,
  The less o' him I never saw.

His legs were but a finger lang,
  And thick and nimle was his knee ;
Between his brows there was a span,
  Between his shoulders ells three.

He lifted a stane sax feet in hight,
　He lifted it up till his right knee ;
And fifty yards and mair, I'm sure,
　I wyte he made the stane to flee.

O little wee man, but ye be wight,
　Tell me whar your dwelling be ;
I hae a bower, compactly built,
　Madam, gin ye'll cum and see.

Sae on we lap, and awa' we rade,
　Till we come to yon little ha' ;
The kipples were o' the gude red gowd,
　The reef was o' the proseyla'.

Pipers were playing, ladies dancing,
　The ladies dancing jimp and sma' ;
At ilka turning o' the spring,
　The little man was wearin's wa'.

Out gat the lights, on cam' the mist,
　Ladies nor mannie mair cou'd see ;
I turn'd about, and gae a look,
　Just at the foot o' Benachie.

The Poor Auld Maidens.

There are three score and ten o' us,
    Puir auld maidens ;
There are three score and ten o' us,
    Puir auld maidens ;
There are three score and ten o' us,
And nae ae penny in our purse ;
Lame, blin', and comfortless,
    Puir auld maidens.

It's very hard we canno' get wed,
    Puir auld maidens ;
It's very hard we canno' get wed,
    Puir auld maidens ;
It's very hard we canno' get wed,
At night fan we gang till our bed,
Naething can be dune or said,
    To comfort auld maidens.

O we are o' a willing min',
    Puir auld maidens ;
O we are o' a willing min',
    Puir auld maidens ;
O we are o' a willing min',
Gin ony man wou'd be sae kin',
As pity us that's lame an' blin',
    Puir auld maidens.

It's very hard we canno' get men,
   Puir auld maidens ;
It's very hard we canno' get men,
   Puir auld maidens ;
It's very hard we canno' get men,
To satisfy a willing min' ;
And pity us that's lame and blin',
   Puir auld maidens.

But O gin we cou'd hae our wish,
   Puir auld maidens ;
But O gin we cou'd hae our wish,
   Puir auld maidens ;
But O gin we cou'd hae our wish,
We'd sing as blythe as ony thrush ;
For something maun be dune for us,
   Puir auld maidens.

But we'll apply to James the third,
   Puir auld maidens ;
But we'll apply to James the third,
   Puir auld maidens ;
But we'll apply to James the third,
And our petition maun be heard,
And for ilk dame a man secur'd,
   To puir auld maidens.

The Guise of Tyrie.

O wat ye how the guise began,
The guise began, the guise began,
O wat ye how the guise began,
 The guise began at Tyrie.

The lady Tyrie and laird o' Glack,
Wha lived baith into the Slack,
Between them twa there was a pack,
 To enter bobbing Andrew.

The muirland wives they're a' gin wud,
They're a' gin wud, they're a' gin wud,
The muirland wives they're a' gin wud,
 For entering bobbing Andrew.
They met the lady in the wauk,
And they began to gie'r ill tauk,
And they began to gie'r ill tauk,
 For entering bobbing Andrew.

They said her husband was in hell,
And she was following fast hersell,
And she was following fast hersell,
 For entering bobbing Andrew.
        The muirland wives, &c.

They tare her veil out ower her tail,
Out ower her tail, out ower her tail,
They tare her veil out ower her tail,
 For entering bobbing Andrew.
        The muirland wives, &c.

Geordy Burnett wi' the gley,
He lay upon Coburty's lay,
He lay upon Coburty's lay
　And beheld the guise o' Tyrie.
　　　The muirland wives, &c.

Gibbie Morrice lay ower the dyke,
And he stirr'd neither man nor tyke,
And he stirr'd neither man nor tyke,
　But beheld the guise o' Tyrie.
　　　The muirland wives, &c.

But Ritchie Gibb, the lady's guard,
He gat a clock for his reward,
He gat a clock for his reward,
　For backing bobbing Andrew.
Then wat ye how the guise began,
The guise began, the guise began,
Then wat ye how the guise began,
　The guise began at Tyrie.

The Fause Lover.

A fair maid sat in her bower door,
　Wringing her lily hands ;
And by it came a sprightly youth,
　Fast tripping o'er the strands.

Where gang ye, young John, she says,
　Sae early in the day ?

It gars me think, by your fast trip,
  Your journey's far away.

He turn'd about wi' surly look,
  And said, What's that to thee?
I'm gaen to see a lovely maid,
  Mair fairer far than ye.

Now hae ye play'd me this, fause love,
  In simmer, mid the flowers?
I sall repay ye back again,
  In winter, 'mid the showers,

But again, dear love, and again, dear love,
  Will ye not turn again?
For as ye look to ither women,
  Shall I to ither men.

Make your choose o' whom you please,
  For I my choice will have;
I've chosen a maid mair fair than thee,
  I never will deceive.

But she's kilt up her claithing fine,
  And after him gaed she;
But aye he said, ye'll turn back,
  Nae farder gang wi' me.

But again, dear love, and again, dear love,
  Will ye never love me again?
Alas! for loving you sae well,
  And you, nae me again.

The first an' town that they came till,
  He bought her brooch and ring ;
But aye he bade her turn again,
  And gang nae farder wi' him.

But again, dear love, and again, dear love,
  Will ye never love me again ?
Alas ! for loving ye sae well,
  And you, nae me again.

The niest an' town that they came till,
  His heart it grew mair fain ;
And he was deep in love wi' her,
  As she was ower again.

The niest an' town that they came till,
  He bought her wedding gown ;
And made her lady o' ha's and bowers,
  In bonny Berwick town.

Our John is Dowing.

I wish that my auld man was dead,
I think my cradle comes nae speed,
I'll get a ranting roving blade,
  To had my cradle rowing.
    Our John is dowing,
    Our John is dowing,
      I'll get a lusty Highlandman
    To had the cradle rowing.

Our Johnny's ta'en the pet,
And aye he's spuing up his meat,
Wi' muckle hoasts and lang spit,
   And he is aye dowing.
      Our John is dowing, &c.

I fell'd my yellow fitted cock,
And stov'd him well into the pot,
And bade him drink the bree o' that,
   But he is aye dowing.
      Our John is dowing, &c.

I gae him skink and fowlie bree,
And ither cordials, twa or three;
But a' these dainties wudna dee,
   For he is aye dowing.
      Our John is dowing,
      Our John is dowing,
      We'll drive him on the gate he's gaen,
      He's better dead than dowing.

Bonny Saint John.

Faer hae ye been, my bonny Saint John,
  Ye've bidden sae lang, ye've bidden sae lang?
Faer hae ye been, my bonny Saint John,
  Ye've bidden sae lang, ye've bidden sae lang?

Up in yon hill, and down in yon glen,
  And I cou'dna win hame, and I cou'dna win hame ;
Now fat will ye gie me unto my supper,
  Now fan I'm come hame, now fan I'm come hame?

A clean dish for you, and a clean spoon,
  For byding sae lang, for byding sae lang ;
A clean dish for you, and a clean spoon,
  For byding sae lang, for byding sae lang.

Robin's Tesment.

Robin rais'd him frae the earth,
  And mounted on a tree ;
O for a clerk to write my will,
  Some time afore I die !

I've biggit on yon bonny burn bank
  Mair than three thousand yearie ;
And fain wou'd I my tesment make,
  If my lanlord wou'd hear me.

Say on, say on, my bonny bird,
  An' see what ye will lea' me ;
For sic a bird as you, Robin,
  Sat never on the brierie.

I lea' to you my bonny cap,
  That sits upo' my head ;
I'll lea' it to yoursell, my lord,
  To drink your wine sae red.

I'll lea' to you my harnpan,
  It is baith lang and sma';
I'll lea' it to yoursell, my lord,
  To drink your wine witha'.

I'll lea' to you my bonny nib,
  That used to stue the corn;
I'll lea' it to yoursell, my lord,
  To be a touting horn.

I'll lea' to you my guid twa een,
  That are like crystal stane;
They will shaw light in a lady's bower,
  When the light o' the day is dane.

I'll lea' to you my twa ribs,
  Which are baith lang and sma';
I'll lea' them to yoursell, my lord,
  For kipples to your ha'.

I'll lea' to you my tee leg,
  Upo' the water o' Wearie;
It will be posts and pillars to you,
  And last this hunner yearie.

I'll lea' to you my tither leg,
  Upo' the water o' Tay;
It will be posts and pillars to you,
  And last for ever and aye.

Ye'll yoke five score o' owsen wanes,
   And hae me to the hill ;
And see ye deal my inmates well,
   And gie the poor their fill.

Poor Robin has his tesment made,
   Upon a stack o' hay ;
But by it came the greedy glade,
   Pu'd Robin quite away.

Then forth it came the weary wren,
   Making a heavy moan ;
Says, Every lady has her lord,
   But my gude lord is gone.

Chorus.—Sing, Father, link ye, hink ye, dink,
     Sing, Father, linkum dearie ;
     Sic a bird as you, Robin,
     Sat never on the brierie.

Richard's Mary.

First whan I came to the north,
   Wi' bonnet blue and belted plaidie,
First I courted a gentleman's oy,
   But now I'm come to Richard's Mary.

First when I came my lassie to woo,
   She was in bed and breakfast ready ;
But up she raise, put on her claise,
   And said she'd been abroad wi'er daddy.

Will ye gie me your daughter, Richard ?
   Will ye gie me your daughter Mary ?
My daughter's a young and tender thing,
   And ye're but a ranting Highland laddie.

The next time I came my lassie to woo,
   She was in bed, her breakfast ready ;
Then up she raise, put on her claise,
   And blinket blythe on her Highland laddie.

Ye'll call your daughter to the door,
   And ye will speak wi' words fu' gadie ;
And see if she is willing to wed,
   Wi' me, that's a brisk young Highland laddie.

He's call'd his daughter to the door,
   And he's spake wi' her words fu' gadie ;
Come tell to me in secret now,
   Gin ye respect yon Highland laddie ?

Tho' I had nought but my coat and smock,
   My tartan gown, and Glasgow plaidie ;
I wou'd brake my bonny tartan gown,
   And make trowsers o't to my Highland laddie.

The bridal it came seen about,
　It wasna lang o' making ready ;
When she was on her high horse set,
　She looked just like ony lady.

When she was in her saddle set,
　And riding in the leys sae bonny ;
Nae pipe nor fiddle gae sic delight
　As she had wi' her ain dear honey.

O fare ye well, Lord Huntly's lands,
　For mony sodger I hae seen ;
But yet I've kept my maidenhead,
　And waured it on my Highland laddie.

As they came by Coberty's yetts,
　Then forth it came her Meg M'Candy ;
Says, Sorrow gang wi' you, ye jolly bridegroom,
　Ye might hae taen me to Gardenstown wi' you !

I wyte I lent you twenty punds,
　O' that I lacked not ae penny ;
But I shall hae it a' again,
　If ye shou'dna hae but Richard's Mary.

O bide ye still, the bride replied,
　Till winter I get my sma' webs ready ;
And ye shall hae it a' again,
　If he shou'dna hae but Richard's Mary.

The bridegroom spake, she's hae as soon,
  O' that she shall not lack ae penny ;
For she shall hae it a' again,
  I've got thrice as muckle wi' you, my Mary.

When they came unto Gardenstown,
  Sae merrily they drank beer and brandy :
And merrily birled the claret wine,
  The sweet sack, and sugar candy.

He wou'dna let her draw her gloves,
  To milk a cow, tho' they had mony ;
But took her in his arms twa,
  Says, They'se a' gang yiel' for you, my Mary.

The Cunning Clerk.

As I gaed down to Collistown,
  Some white fish for to buy, buy,
The cunning clerk he followed me,
  And he followed me speedily, ly,
  And he followed me speedily.

Says, Faur ye gaun, my dearest dear ?
  O faur ye gaun, my dow, dow ?
There's naebody comes to my bedside,
  And naebody wins to you, you,
  And naebody wins to you.

Your brother is a gallant square wright,
 A gallant square wright is he, he ;
Ye'll gar him make a lang ladder,
 Wi' thirty steps and three, three,
 Wi' thirty steps and three.

And gar him big a deep, deep creel,
 A deep creel and a string, string ;
And ye'll come up to my bedside,
 And come bonnily linken in, in,
 And come bonnily linken in.

The auld gudeman and auld gudewife,
 To bed they went to sleep, sleep ;
But wae mat worth the auld gudewife,
 A wink she cou'dna get, get,
 A wink she cou'dna get.

I dream'd a dreary dream this night,
 I wish it binna true, true,
That the rottens had come thro' the wa',
 And cutted the coverin' blue, blue,
 And cutted the coverin' blue.

Then up it raise the auld gudeman,
 To see gin it was true, true ;
And he's gane to his daughter dear,
 Says, What are ye doing, my dow, dow ?
 Says, What are ye doing, my dow ?

What are ye doing, my daughter dear ?
  What are ye doing, my dow, dow ?
The prayer book's in my hand, father,
    Praying for my auld minnie and you, you,
    Praying for my auld minnie and you.

The auld gudeman and auld gudewife,
    To bed they went to sleep, sleep ;
But wae mat worth the auld gudewife,
    But aye she waken'd yet, yet,
    But aye she waken'd yet.

I dream'd a dreary dream this night,
    I wish it binna true, true,
That the cunning clerk and your ae daughter
    Were aneath the coverin' blue, blue,
    Were aneath the coverin' blue.

O rise yoursell, gudewife, he says,
    The diel may had you fast, fast ;
Atween you and your ae daughter
    I canno' get ae night's rest, rest,
    I canno' get ae night's rest.

Up then raise the auld gudewife,
    To see gin it was true, true ;
And she fell arselins in the creel,
    And up the string they drew, drew,
    And up the string they drew.

Win up, win up, gudeman, she says,
  Win up, and help me now, now ;
For he that ye gae me to last night,
  I think he's catch'd me now, now,
  I think he's catch'd me now.

Gin auld Nick he has catch'd you now,
  I wish he may had you fast, fast ;
As for you and your ae daughter,
  I never get kindly rest, rest,
  I never get kindly rest.

They howded her, and they showded her,
  Till the auld wife gat a fa', fa' ;
And three ribs o' the auld wife's side
  Gaed knip, knap, ower in twa, twa,
  Gaed knip, knap, ower in twa.

The Clerks of Oxenford.

I'll tell you a tale, or I'll sing you a song,
  Will grieve your heart full sair ;
How the twa bonny clerks o' Oxenford
  Went aff to learn their lear.

Their father lov'd them very weel,
  Their mother muckle mair ;
And sent them on to Billsbury,
  To learn deeper lear.

Then out it spake their mother dear,
  Do weel my sons, do weel ;
And haunt not wi' the young women,
  Wi' them to play the fiel.

Their father sware them on their souls,
  Their mother on their life,
Never to lie wi' the auld mayor's daughters,
  Nor kiss the young mayor's wife.

But they hadna been in Billsbury
  A twallmonth and a day,
Till the twa bonny clerks o' Oxenford
  With the mayor's twa daughters lay.

As these twa clerks they sat and wrote,
  The ladies sewed and sang ;
There was mair mirth in that chamber
  Than all fair Ferrol's land.

But word's gane to the wicked mayor,
  As he sat at the wine,
That the twa bonny clerks o' Oxenford
  With his twa daughters had lyne.

O have they lain with my daughters dear,
  Heirs out ower a' my land ?
The morn, ere I eat or drink,
  I'll hang them with my hand.

Then he has ta'en the twa bonny clerks,
   Bound them frae tap to tae,
Till the reddest blood in their body
   Out ower their nails did gae.

Whare will I get a little wee boy
   Will win gowd to his fee ;
That will rin on to Oxenford,
   And that right speedilie ?

Then up it starts a bonny boy,
   Gold yellow was his hair ;
I wish his father and mother joy,
   His true love muckle mair.

Says, Here am I, a little wee boy,
   Will win gowd to my fee,
That will rin on to Oxenford,
   And that right speedilie.

Where ye find the grass green growing,
   Set down your heel and rin ;
And where ye find the brigs broken,
   Ye'll bend your bow and swim.

But when ye come to Oxenford,
   Bide neither to chap nor ca' ;
But set your bent bow to your breast,
   And lightly loup the wa'.

Where he found the grass green growing,
  He slack't his shoes and ran ;
And where he found the brigs broken,
  He bent his bow and swam.

And when he came to Oxenford,
  Did neither chap nor ca' ;
But set his bent bow to his breast,
  And lightly leapt the wa'.

What news, what news, my little wee boy ?
  What news hae ye to me ?
How are my sons in Billsbury,
  Since they went far frae me ?

Your sons are well, and learning well,
  But at a higher school ;
And ye'll never see your sons again,
  On the holy days o' Yule.

Wi' sorrow now gae make my bed,
  Wi' care and caution lay me down ;
That man on earth shall ne'er be born,
  Shall see me mair gang on the groun'.

Take twenty pounds in your pocket,
  And ten and ten to tell them wi' ;
And gin ye getna hynde Henry,
  Bring ye gay Gilbert hame to me.

Out it speaks old Oxenford,
  A sorry, sorry man, was he ;
Your strange wish does me surprise,
  They are baith there alike to me.

Wi' sorrow now I'll saddle my horse,
  And I will gar my bridle ring ;
And I shall be at Billsbury,
  Before the small birds sweetly sing.

Then sweetly sang the nightingale
  As she sat on the wand ;
But sair, sair, mourn'd Oxenford,
  As he gaed in the strand.

When he came to Billsbury,
  He rade it round about ;
And at a little shott window
  His sons were looking out.

O lye ye there, my sons, he said,
  For oxen, or for kye ?
Or, is it for a little o' deep dear love,
  Sae sair bound as ye lye ?

We lye not here, father, they said,
  For oxen, nor for kye ;
It's all for a little o' deep dear love,
  Sae sair bound as we lye.

O borrow's, borrow's, father, they said,
   For the love we bear to thee !
O never fear, my pretty sons,
   Well borrowed ye shall be.

Then he's gane to the wicked mayor,
   And hailed him courteouslie ;
Good day, good day, oh Billsbury,
   God make you safe and free !—
Come sit you down, brave Oxenford,
   What are your wills with me ?

Will ye gie me my sons again,
   For gold, or yet for fee ?
Will ye gie me my sons again,
   For's sake that died on tree ?

I winna gie you your sons again,
   For gold, nor yet for fee ;
But if ye'll stay a little while,
   Ye'se see them hanged hie.

Ben it came the mayor's daughters,
   Wi' kirtle, coat alone ;
Their eyes did sparkle like the gold,
   As they tript on the stone.

Will ye gie us our loves, father,
   For gold, or yet for fee ?
Or will ye take our own sweet life,
   And let our true loves be ?

He's ta'en a whip into his hand,
   And lash'd them wond'rous sair ;
Gae to your bowers, ye vile rank whores,
   Ye'se never see them mair.

Then out it speaks old Oxenford,
   A sorry man was he ;
Gang to your bowers, ye lily flowers,
   For a' this maunna be.

Out it speaks him hynde Henry,
   Come here, Janet, to me ;
Will ye gie me my faith and troth,
   And love, as I gae thee ?

Ye shall hae your faith and troth,
   Wi' God's blessing and mine ;
And twenty times she kiss'd his mouth,
   Her father looking on.

Then out it speaks him gay Gilbert,
   Come here, Margaret, to me ;
Will ye gie me my faith and troth,
   And love, as I gae thee ?

Yes, ye shall get your faith and troth,
   Wi' God's blessing and mine ;
And twenty times she kiss'd his mouth,
   Her father looking on.

Ye'll take aff your twa black hats,
   Lay them down on a stone,
That nane may ken that ye are clerks
   Till ye are putten down.

The bonny clerks they died that morn,
   Their loves died lang ere noon ;
Their father and mother for sorrow died,—
   They all died very soon.

These six souls went up to heaven,
   (I wish sae may we a' !)
The mighty mayor went down to hell,
   For wrong justice and law.

NOTES.

SIR PATRICK SPENS.

Page 1.

THIS old and justly esteemed ballad has given rise to much antiquarian conjecture, and critical research. It appears to have been first published by Dr. Percy, in his Reliques of Ancient English Poetry, in 1757, as a Scottish Ballad ; and in this imperfect state it has been republished in almost every subsequent collection of ancient ballads, occasionally with variations and additions. Sir Walter Scott, who has also given an edition of it in the Minstrelsy of the Border, admits it to be but a fragment. A complete copy was therefore a great desideratum in the literary world, at least to that part of it who have made it their study to rescue from the devouring hand of time those graphic reliques of our early ancestors. History has been silent on the particular event which gave rise to its composition, if we except a few indirect hints by some of the old chroniclers, which have made almost every editor have a different opinion of its origin. The present version, therefore, may supply a *desideratum* in the annals of Scottish Song, which has hitherto been so often attempted by the ingenious and the learned in vain. It was taken down from the recitation of "a wight of Homer's craft ;" who, as a wandering minstrel, blind from his infancy, has been travelling in the North as a mendicant for these last fifty years. He learned it in his youth from a very old person, and the words are exactly as recited, free from those emendations which have ruined so many of our best Scottish Ballads. The subject on which the ballad is founded is thus related

by Hector Boece, in his Chronicles of Scotland :—"And for
the mair corboration of perseuerand amyte and kyndness be-
tuix Scottis and Danis in tymes cumyng, Margaret, Kyng
Alexanderis dochter, hauand bot ane zeir in age sal be giuin in
marriage to Haningo ye son of kyng Magnus quhen scho is
cumyn to perfit age." This marriage took place betwixt the
king of Scotland's daughter, Margaret, and the king of Norway's son, Haningo, about the year 1270. The current report
is, that Sir Patrick was sent on an Embassy to Norway to
bring home Margaret, grand-daughter of Alexander III. king
of Scotland, which appears to me to be inconsistent with the
tenor and narrative of the ballad. From the following verse,
I am more inclined to believe that Sir Patrick, accompanied
with five-and-fifty Scots lords' sons, were destined to carry
to the court of Norway its chosen queen, and not to bring
from that court a queen for Scotland.

> But I maun sail the seas the morn,
>   An' likewise sae maun you ;—
> To Norway, wi' our king's daughter,—
>   A chosen queen she's now.

It would also appear, from the first line of this verse, that the
ship had been in readiness for the voyage, as she was to sail
on the day after the orders had arrived, and not that she had
been prohibited by an act of parliament to sail during the
winter months. However, the season of the year is not speci-
fied here.

YOUNG AKIN.

Page 6.

In some late publications, I have seen fragments of this
beautiful ballad under various names.—It is now for the first
time given in a complete state.

The ballad is, to all appearance, very old ; and agrees with
the romantic history and times of Fergus II. It will be con-
sidered by all lovers of Scottish Song, as a great acquisition
to their store of traditionary poetry. The heroine, Lady

Margaret, a king's daughter, was stolen by her father's cup-
bearer, who built for her a bower, in which she was so artfully
confined, that no one could have discovered the place of her
residence. In this bower, she bare to her adopted husband
seven sons, the oldest of whom was the means of releasing her
from her dreary abode. On his arrival at the court of his grand-
father, whither he had gone to reconnoitre, the old monarch
at once perceived such a family likeness in the face of this
woodland boy, as made him enquire after the fate of his
long lost daughter. She, with the rest of her sons, arrived
at her father's palace ; and like the prodigal, or long lost son,
was welcomed with joy and gladness. The ballad concludes
with the pardon of Young Akin,—his reception at the king's
court, and the baptism of the children.

YOUNG WATERS.
Page 15.

A mutilated edition of this beautiful old ballad was first published by Lady Jean Hume, sister to the Earl of Hume, while re-
siding in Glasgow. It has been copied into a great many collections of Ancient Ballads since. The version which is here given
to the public, is the only complete one with which I have ever
met. It contains a history of the whole transaction, although
in one case, under a fictitious name. I am, however, inclined to
think, that Young Waters was David Graham of Fintray, who
was found guilty and beheaded the 16th February 1592, for
being concerned in a Popish plot :—the particulars of which
are to be found recorded in Spotswood's History, page 391.

THE GOWANS SAE GAY.
Page 22.

A ballad somewhat similar in fancy, was published by
Allan Ramsay in his Tea Table Miscellany ; but it differs
widely in romantic fiction and narrative from the present,
whose hero is an Elfin-knight, with whom the heroine falls in
love on hearing the sound of his horn. Great deeds are said

to be done on the first morning of May, such as gathering dew
before the sun arise ; which is an infallible cosmetic for the
ladies.   The two following verses, on the virtue of May-
dew, are from the ballad alluded to.

> O lady fair, what do you here ?
>   There gowans are gay.
> Gathering the dew, what need ye spier ?
>   The first morning of May.

> The dew, quoth I, what can that mean ?
>   There gowans are gay.
> Quoth she, to wash my mistress clean,
>   The first morning of May.

The lady seems to have been a match for the fairy ; for, by
her syren song, like Judith with Holoferness, she lulled him
asleep in her lap, and afterwards cut off his head with his
own weapon.

THE TWA MAGICIANS.
Page 24.

There is a novelty in this legendary ballad very amusing,
and it must be very old.—I never saw anything in print which
had the smallest resemblance to it.   The singular metamor-
phoses, and curious transformations of the hero and heroine
of the ballad by the art of magic, are truly novel.   Magic can
accomplish great·things, either by natural or supernatural
means.

Magic is divided into Natural, Artificial, and Diabolical.
Natural magic produces extraordinary and marvellous
effects, by the mere force of natural means.   Artificial magic produces also extraordinary and marvellous effects,
by human industry and wit ; as, the glass sphere of Archi-
medes ; the wooden pigeon of Architas ; the golden birds
of the Emperor of Leo, which sung ; Boetius's brazen ones,
which did both sing and fly, and serpents of the same metal,
which did hiss ; and Albert le Grand's speaking head, &c.
Diabolical magic, or the black art, hath surprising effects,

surpassing those of art or nature, by the help of Demons: as
Pharaoh's magicians, who did imitate the true miracles of
God. And in the last age there was a magician, who made
the dead corps of a famous harper at Bologne walk and play,
as if he had been alive, by a charm which he put under one
of its arm-pits. Gasparus Peucerus, the physician, who
mentions this, says, that another magician, who discovered
the cause of this, did take out the charm with great dexterity;
so that the corps fell to the ground, and remained immoveable,
Isidore, Bishop of Seville, says, that the magicians did move
the elements; kill men by their very charms, without poison;
and raise the devil, from whom they learnt how to annoy their
enemies. Natural and artificial magic have no charm in
them, if people take care not to awaken a spirit of curiosity,
and press too far into futurities and superstitious enquiries;
but as for the black art, 'tis always unlawful, as employing a
correspondence with evil spirits. There are some people, who
either disbelieve, or pretend to do so, that there is any such
thing as witches; but this is a truth, to say nothing more,
which no man, who believes anything in revealed religion, can
call in question; for the Holy Scriptures, in several places,
forbids us to have recourse to magicians; and mentions those
made use of by Pharaoh and Manasses; of the witch of
Endor, consulted by Saul; of Simon and Bar-Jesu, magicians;
and of a woman who had a familiar spirit dispossessed by
Saint Paul; all mentioned in the Acts of the Apostles. The
councils likewise excommunicate magicians, and the Holy
Fathers mention them upon occasion : neither is the civil law
wanting in penal provisions against them . there is likewise
a statute in the beginning of the reign of King James I. which
makes witchcraft felony. — *Thier's Treatise of Superstitions.*

CHILDE OWLET.

Page 27.

Lady Erskine appears to have been a daughter of one of the
Earls of Marr, who disdained to take the title of her husband

as being below her degree. Although he is here called a
Lord, it does not always prove that those were Lords of
Parliament, or noblemen, who were called so, but merely
given as a title of courtesy. It is quite a common thing for a
lady who wishes to honour her husband, to call him lord.
Sarah called Abraham lord, and was accounted a worthy
woman for so doing. Childe Owlet was an illegitimate son of
Lord Ronald's sister, who had been brought up in the house
of his uncle, under a fictitious name ; but, like another Joseph,
chose rather to suffer death than be ungrateful to his
guardian, or dishonour his preserver's bed.

THE BENT SAE BROWN.

Page 30.

Love, says the preacher, is as strong as death. Our old
poesy is fraught with tales of wonder, as well as delight. The
love which is displayed by the lady in this ballad is passing
human comprehension. It is the strongest passion, and one
which betrays reason and reflection, and to whose shrine
almost all have been made to bow. A few centuries ago, love
signified an invincible inclination, as may be seen by the
present ballad. It has, however, in the present case, another
meaning. What lady in this enlightened age of refinement
and morals, would sacrifice the life of three brothers, and
incur the deadly hate of a fond father and an indulgent
mother, for the gratification of saving the life of a knightly
gallant, as here depicted ? The stratagem which the old
woman falls upon for the punishment of the young knight,
proves abortive. The king, to whom she made her complaint,
was much better pleased with the artless simplicity of the
daughter's statement of the murder, who had also gone to the
king to crave pardon for her lover's manslaughter, as it may
be termed, being in self-defence. From her familiarity with
the sovereign, I am led to suppose she had been a woman of
high degree ; for we are informed, she took him in her arms,
and kissed him cheek and chin.

LEESOME BRAND.
Page 38.

I am quite unprepared to say where that land is "where winds never blow, nor cocks ever crow," unless I make it Fairyland. In fact, the tenor of the whole ballad authorizes me to think it so. It would also seem that Leesome Brand's mother had been an old enchantress ; for, by three drops of Saint Paul's blood, which she had kept in a gray horn, beneath her head, she restored to life his wife and child.

CLERK TAMAS.
Page 43.

This ballad bears all the characteristics of antiquity. It seems rather of a romantic kind, although in many places allegorical.

THE QUEEN OF SCOTLAND.
Page 45.

Whether this ballad alludes to Mary queen of Scotland's illicit amours, which were so notorious, I leave my readers to judge. It is evident, however, like the wife of Potiphar, she contrived the death of this chaste young man, who acted a more honourable part than defile the bed of his royal master. The young woman, by whose instrumentality his life had been prolonged, he married, as a proof of his gratitude : and Providence, willing to encourage such virtuous actions, healed the wound the serpent had made.

THE EARL OF MAR'S DAUGHTER.
Page 48.

In the oriental courts of the ancients, magic was a favourite study, and formed part of the education of their nobles, which they brought to great perfection ; I mean to such perfection as this science is capable of being brought by human means. Till within these few years past, a belief in magic and witchcraft was cherished, not only by the ignorant but the learned

in our own country. In Toledo, Seville, and Salamanca, and
in various parts of Italy, there were public schools, where
magic was taught.   At one period, it was customary for the
noblemen and gentlemen of Scotland to finish their education
by making what was called the tour of Europe, and attending
for a short period one of those eastern seminaries of darkness.
Transformations were common in the days of Ovid ; men were
metamorphosed into birds, beasts, fishes, woods, and water.
The Arabian, Tartarian, Eastern, and Fairy Tales, furnish us
with abundance of instances of this kind, charms having been
used for the purpose.   Scotland, till of late, had her witches,
her warlocks, her fairies, her brownies, and a hundred more
supernatural and midnight visitors, who were capable of riding through the air on broomsticks, or crossing the raging
ocean in egg-shells, or sieves, as happens, which may be seen
at full length in Satan's Invisible World Discovered.   The
Earl of Gowrie was said to be a staunch advocate for charms,
amulets, and Homerical medicines, as mentioned in the Gowrie
Conspiracy.   "When he, i.e., Earl Gowrie, went to Padua,
there he studied Necromancy : his own pedagogue master
Rhind testifies, that he had these characters aye upon him,
which he loved so, that if he had forgot to put them in his
breeches, he would run up and down like a madman, and he
had them upon him when he was slain ; and as they testify
that saw it, he could not bleed so long as they were upon
him."   Many are the instances, even to this day, of charms
practised among the vulgar, especially in the Highlands,
attended with forms of prayer.

   This ballad has the highest claim to antiquity. The learned
Lord Hailes says, the title of Marr is one of the earldoms
whose origin is lost in its antiquity ; it would therefore be
vain for me to ascribe the date of the ballad to any precise
period.

THE DEATH OF LORD WARRISTON,
Page 55.

   In another note, I have endeavoured to shew, that the title
of lord is sometimes conferred on the proprietor of a small

estate. In the present case, I have seen two different ballads, one published by Mr Jamieson, vol. i. p. 109 of his Popular Ballads ; another by Mr Kinloch, p. 49 of his Ancient Scottish Ballads ;—in both he is called the Laird of Warieston. The copy given here is the completest of the three, and changes the cause of the melancholy catastrophe altogether. The ballad, as most of our ancient Scottish ballads are, is founded on fact, and is very old, as may be seen by consulting Birrel's Diary, pages, 49 and 61, from which the following extracts are given :—

" 1600, July 2.—The same 2 day, Kinkaid of Wariston, murderet be his awin wyff and servant man, and her nurische being also upon the conspiracy. The said gentilwoman being apprehendit, scho was tane to the Girth crosse upon the 5 day of Julii, and her heid struck fra her bodie at the Cannagait fit, quha diet verie patiently. Her nurische was brunt at the same time, at 4 houris in the morneing, the 5 of Julii.

" The 16 of Junii (1603) Robert Weir broken on ane cart wheel with ane coulter of ane pleuch, in the hand of the hangman, for murdering the gudeman of Warriston, quhilk he did 2 Julii 1600."

I also give the following excerpt from an old MS. of curious Trials of the Court of Justiciary, as it differs somewhat from the account given of this diabolical murder in Birrel's Diary, as stated above.

" 1604, June 26.—William Weir delaytet of art and part of the cruel murder of John Kincaid of Warrieston, in anno 1600. The part of this barbarous murder is this ;—Jean Liuingston, spouse to the said John Kincaid, having conceived a deadly hatred towards her husband for alledged maletreatment, did send Janet Murdo, her nurse, to the said William Weir, and implored him to murder her husband ; who accordingly was brought to Warrieston, and about midnight they came into the room where he was lying in bed, and being wakened with the noice, called to him, whereupon, the said Weir, running to him, and with a severe stroke with his hand, struck him on the wein organ, and thereby he fell out of his bed on the floor, whereupon Weir struck him on the belly with his feet, and thereafter gripped him by the throat, and held him till he strangled him to death.

" It does not appear how proved, nor if the lady and nurse were tried, but the Jury having found him guilty, he was sentenced to be broken alive on the row, or wheel, and be exposed thereon for twenty-four hours ; and thereafter the said row, with the body on it, to be placed between Leith and Warrieston, till orders be given to burn the body."

EARL CRAWFORD.
Page 60.

Lindsay, one of the Earls of Crawford, having married a daughter of———of Stobhall in Aberdeenshire, unwittingly took as an affront, a jesting word this lady said regarding her son. The story of the lady's fatality, is told by herself, in very pathetic strains. The ballad concludes with the death of both. Those of the surname of Lindsay, at one period, were very numerous in Scotland, having spread into numerous branches. The name was derived from the manor of Lindsay in Essex, and consequently of English origin.

ROSE THE RED AND WHITE LILLIE.
Page 66.

A ballad of this name, but considerably different from the present, appeared in ᵗʰe Border Minstrelsy, vol. ii. p. 444. The editor of that esteemed work, thinks it may have originally related to the history of the celebrated Robin Hood. The hero of this piece is of Scottish extraction, and consequently not the same personage. The place from whence these ladies made their escape, as narrated in the ballad, was Anster town, in the county of Fife.

BURD ISBEL AND SIR PATRICK.
Page 75.

It is not an uncommon thing, even in the present day,

to find a person who will mis-swear himself to half-a-dozen of young women in a year; particularly to those whom they consider in a state incapable of retaliating, as was the case with Burd Isbel. None but those destitute of every sense of honour would be guilty of such injustice to a young and unprotected female, who rather merits their kindest sympathy. The last verse of this ballad would cause the reader to think the forsaken maid had the power of anathematizing her mis-sworn knight, for the selling of his precious soul.

CHARLIE M'PHERSON.
Page 84.

Under the feudal law, a Highland chieftain was invested with more power and authority than many democratic king, and made use of it according to the strength of his clan, and his own arbitrary or tyrannical disposition. To rob and despoil parents of their only daughter, on whom they looked for comfort in their declining years, and carry her off, they knew not whither, was not one of the worst actions of which some of them were guilty; but, like the Romish Inquisition, no one durst say it was wrong which they had done, unless their strength and power were such as to be able to overcome them in battle.

Charles M'Pherson was one of that Highland clan, commonly called the Clan-Cattan, famed for antiquity and valour. They draw their original from the Chatti, or Catti, the ancient inhabitants of Hessia and Thuringia in Germany, whence they were expelled by the Hermondures, with the assistance of the Romans, in the reign of the Emperor Tiberius. Cattorum Castellum, one of the Landgrave of Hesse's palaces, and Cattorum Melibæci, or Catzenellebogen, which is one of the family's titles, do still preserve the memory of the ancient Catti; who being forced to leave their country, came lower down upon the Rhine into Battavia, now Holland, where Catwick still bears their name; thence a colony of them came into Scotland, and landing in the north of that kingdom, were kindly received by the king of Scots, who gave them that part of the country where they landed, which from them was called Caithness, *i. e.*, the Cattie's corner; being settled here, they did many eminent services against the Picts, and other enemies of the Scots, till the time of King Alphinus, when the chief of the Catti, called Gilly Cattan Moir, *i. e.*, the Great, for his extraordinary conduct and valour, being married to a sister of Brudus, king of the Picts, he was in a strait how to behave himself betwixt both kings, who, in a little time after, fell out, and as the expedient, resolves upon a neutrality. In the reign of Kennethus II., who also had war with the Picts, this Gilly Cattan Moir, amongst others of the Scotch nobility, was summoned to attend the king's standard, he excused himself, by reason of his age; but to evidence his loyalty, though allied to the Picts, he sent one of his sons, with half of his clan, to join the Scots, which did not a little contribute to that fatal blow, which issued in the utter ruin of the Picts. Most of the Clan Chattan, with their valiant leader, falling in the battle, the old man died of grief, and the remaining part were, by the advice of their enemies, prosecuted as favourers of the Picts, expelled Caithness, and, with much ado, obtained leave to settle in Lochaber, where they remain to this day.

There are many other Highland families, whose name begins with M' or M'Mac, which signifies the son of such a man, who being eminent for some great thing, his posterity chose his name, or surname, as the M'Leans, M'Intoshes, &c.

CHARLES GRÆME.

Page 87.

There seems to be a very great inconsistency manifested throughout the whole of this ballad in the lady's behaviour towards the ghost of her departed lover. Perhaps she wished to sit and sigh alone, undisturbed with visits from the inhabitants of the grave. On her first outset, she was to sit and harp on his grave a twelvemonth and a day; but after the first night, we hear no more of her harping.

THE COURTEOUS KNIGHT.
Page 89.

A ballad similar in incident, but greatly deficient in narrative, under the title of "Proud Lady Margaret," is printed in the 2d vol. p. 250² of the Border Minstrelsy.

SWEET WILLIE AND FAIR MAISRY.
Page 95.

Mr Finlay, in the note to "Sweet Willie," a mutilated copy, in his Collection, vol. ii. p. 61, says,—"This ballad has had the misfortune, in common with many others, of being much mutilated by reciters. I have endeavoured, by the assistance of some fragments, to make it as complete as possible." Mr Finlay has, however, for all his painful industry, come far short of completing or perfecting the ballad, as may be seen by comparing it with this copy, which, I think, is the only genuine one yet published. In the 139th page of the "Minstrelsy Ancient and Modern," edited by my worthy friend, William Motherwell, Esq., I find another version of this ballad, considerably different from this one, under the title of "Fair Janet;" taken, as he says, from a "Ballad Book," edited by Mr Charles Kirkpatrick Sharpe, and enlarged by three stanzas from the ballads of "Willie and Annet" and "Sweet Willie." The copy I have here given is, like all the others in this Collection, indebted to no printed copy whatever.

YOUNG PRINCE JAMES.
Page 101.

An imperfect ballad, under the name of "Lady Maisry," is given in Mr Jamieson's Collection, vol. i. p. 73, without note or comment, and has subsequently appeared in Gilchrist's

Collection, and the Minstrelsy Ancient and Modern, in the
same state. The catastrophe is somewhat similar to that of
Young Prince James. Instead of Lord William, as in Mr
Jamieson's copy, we are informed, the hero of the piece was
young Prince James ; and may have been James Stewart,
afterwards king of Scotland, who was at that time a prisoner
in England, but had come to Scotland in the disguise of an
English Baron.

BROWN ROBYN'S CONFESSION.
Page 108.

This ballad has probably been written by one of the Bene-
dictine Monks, who settled in England in the year 596, in
the dark ages of Roman Catholic superstition, to enforce
upon his silly-minded hearers the real, or pretended advan-
tages arising from auricular confession. Surely none of my
readers are so grossly ignorant as to be made to believe, that
the mere confession of a crime, particularly that of incest,
and of such hideous magnitude as the one here narrated,
would entitle any one to a pardon of the same.

THE THREE BROTHERS.
Page 109.

In my weary, though pleasant researches among the inhabitants of the straw-thatched cottages that abound in Aberdeenshire, I have found two different copies of this ballad, both
of which differ from the two given by Sir Walter Scott, under
the titles of "Archie of Ca'field, and Jock o' the Side." One
of the two recovered by me, I sent to the editor of Minstrelsy
Ancient and Modern, where it was printed, under the title
of "Billie Archie," in the 335th page of that very valuable
work. There is a quaintness, a cunning, a bravery, and a
degree of honour displayed in this ballad, which the reader
will admire. The cowardice of little Dick, and the spirited
manliness of Johnny Ha, at the swimming of Annan water,
are finely contrasted. We may suppose this ballad to have

been written about the year 1597, as at that time Johnny Ha, *alias* John Hall of Newbigging, is mentioned in the list of clans who infested the Border.

THE MAID AND FAIRY.
Page 114.

This is one of the many beautiful legendary chants that are to be found in the nursery, which are said and sung to amuse fretful children. The Genii, or Spirit, that presides over the "Wells sae Weary," is often introduced by the ancients in their tales and songs of wonder and delight. It was with wells, as it was with churches, in the darkened ages of superstition; every well had its name and tutelar deity, to which it was dedicated, and offerings made, as it was supposed such gave the waters those balsamic and healing qualities for which many of them were so much renowned. These wells were held in the greatest veneration by those who frequented them, and often the place where lovers met to pledge their faith and troth. This charming little piece is undoubtedly very old, as a stanza of one of a similar aspect appears in the Complaynt of Scotland, p. 234. The subject is as follows :—An old woman and her daughter lived in a remote part of the country, far from the haunts of busy men; when, it so happened, one wintry night, that the maid was sent to the "Well sae Weary" for two jars of water. With much reluctance she went, having, as she said, gone frequently before, and found nothing but mud in a puddle. The old woman, however, was not to be put off with such silly excuses, but, in a harsher tone of voice, and more peremptorily, commanded her daughter to go that instant. The order was imperative, so she complied with reluctance. When at the well, mumbling some anathematizing language against her mother, the Spirit of the Well appeared, who proffered his assistance in finding pure water for her, provided she would admit him into her dwelling when night was farer advanced. She did so, came home with her water, and met with a gruff reception from her mother. Shortly after

appeared the Genii at the door, singing the first four lines of
the song, and was admitted.   In the second four lines, he
craves, as his due, the castick, or stem, having had coleworts
for their supper, a dish common to the peasantry of Scotland.
In the third four lines, he asks his brose, (oatmeal, and the
decoction of the coleworts stirred together;) in the fourth four
lines, he requests the kale ; and in the fifth four lines, he
petitions the maid to lay him down in a bed, putting her in
mind, at the same time, of the favour he had done her at the
Well sae Weary.   The old woman, who, ere now, had been
a silent spectator to all that was passing, got enraged, and
commanded her daughter to throw him out of the house,
which was instantly done.   The sixth and last four lines
conclude the piece with his prayers or malison for her woe,
and an opportunity of having her again in his power at the
Wells sae Weary.

YOUNG HUNTING.
Page 116.

Fragments of this enchanting ballad have been printed in
various collections, under a variety of titles.   In Wother-
spoon's Collection, vol. i. p. 148, are to be found seven
mutilated verses ; and in Lawrie and Symington's Collection,
vol. i. p. 184, are five verses, all of which make the hero of
the piece Earl Richard.   Sir Walter Scott has also given two
ballads in the 2d volume of the Minstrelsy of the Scottish
Border under the titles of "Lord William," and "Earl
Richard," which are much like Young Hunting in detail.
Sir Walter supposes the one to have been derived from the
other.   In his note to Earl Richard, he says, "There are
two ballads in Mr Herd's MSS. upon the following story, in
one of which the unfortunate knight is termed "Young
Huntin."   In Mr Kinloch's Scottish Ballads, is one under
the name of "Young Redin ;" but he is of opinion that it
differs essentially, both in incident and detail, from either
Lord William or Earl Richard.   I am, however, inclined to
think, its author has been indebted to Young Hunting for his

plot. Young Hunting, though last on the stage of public criticism, is not the least in poetical merit ;—it is superior to all those which have preceded it, and now for the first time printed in a complete and perfect state, with beauties that are not to be found in any of the other fragments.

BLANCHEFLOUR AND JELLYFLORICE.
Page 122.

There is a very old romance of this name, from which I suspect some less inspired poetaster than its real author, has taken the present ballad, modelled it in his old mould, and modernized it to suit the climate of his own times. A young woman who had wearied in the employment of her former mistress, goes to better her fortune, in pursuit of new adventures ; when she arrived at the palace of a queen, where she was admitted, but warned to beware of the queen's son. She, however, soon forgot her mistress's advice, and grew fond of the young prince, and admitted him to make love and pay his addresses to her, which gave great offence to the queen, who ordered her to undergo a severe punishment : but from this she was soon released, and married by the prince.

LADY ISABEL.
Page 126.

Some stepmothers prove the bane of bitterness to their husband's former offspring, when they have it in their power. Every trifling thing is an excuse for their cruelty. The gowns which were sent to Lady Isabel from her lover beyond seas, were made a plea for her stepmother to wreak her vengeance upon. In short, every thing militates against the young and the fair ; and she gave her poison to drink, under the mask of friendship, although not unknown to the young lady. From the circumstance of Lady Isabel's mother appearing to her in the quire of Mary's Kirk, we may suppose the ancients had an idea that the souls of the departed knew, and were conversant with the affairs of the world which they had left. Indeed, almost all their writings sanction this belief.

GIGHT'S LADY.

Page 130.

Like many of our best ballads, "Gight's Lady," or, as in another edition of it,—"Geordie," it has suffered great y in the hands of ballad collectors. In fact, all the other editions of this ballad I have met with, have been deprived of their original beauty and catastrophe, by the too officious, and sacrilegious hands of our wise-headed modern reciters and interpolaters. It came first through the hands of Burns, who sent it to "Johnston's Museum," where it first appeared in an incomplete state. Qualified as Burns was to make new ones, he has in many instances, been very unsuccessful in mending old; and I much fear this one has not been much improved: for, as the link-boy said to Pope the poet, who was a crooked mis-shapen creature, when he prayed to God to mend him, that it would be much easier for God to make two new ones, than to mend him. This ballad, which is now for the first time published complete, is quite at variance with all its printed predecessors. Mr Cunningham says,— "The genuine old song relates to some forgotten feud between the powerful Gordons and Hays." This is quite incorrect; as Mr C. could never have seen the genuine old song of which he speaks, or he would at once have perceived it had no reference or connection whatever with the feud that once existed between the Earls of Huntly and Errol, as mentioned at full length by Gordon, in his History of the Gordons. The genuine old ballad was composed upon quite another incident, and recounts an affair which actually took place in the reign or rather minority of King James VI. Sir George Gordon of Gight, had become too familiar with the laird of Bignet's lady, for which the former was imprisoned, and likely to lose his life; but for the timely interference of Lady Anne, his lawful spouse, who came to Edinburgh to plead his cause, which she did with success,—gained his life, and was

rewarded with the loss of her own, by the hand of her ungrateful husband. William Gordon, who writes the history
of his own name, in order to palliate as much as possible
every act of the Gordons, says, that Sir George Gordon of
Gight went over to France, either for recreation, or to eschew
the exorbitant authority of the regent, who was a violent
enemy, not only to him, but to all the name of Gordon."
This seems to be a very plausible way of warding off the dis-
grace of a murder, but it will not do.—He fled to save his life
for the murder of his lady. Any one will see what puerile and
indefinite reasons Gordon gives for his client's going abroad.
In fact, he is not certain of the cause himself ; for it will be
observed, he says,—"*either* for recreation, or *to eschew* the
exorbitant authority of the regent,"&c. Mr Ritson gives a
version of this ballad, different from all the others, composed
in 1610.

THE DROWNED LOVERS.
Page 137.

A fragment of this ballad, under the name of " Willie and
May Margaret," appeared in Mr Jamieson's Collection, vol.
i. p. 135, where he says, "it was taken from the recitation
of Mrs Brown of Falkland." I have now, for the first time,
given it in a complete state, which exhibits those tragical
ends, which are so consistent with the wrath and malice of
an enraged mother. The unfortunate visit was fatal to both
lovers ; for, like Lord Gregory's mother, the maid's mother
betrayed both, which ended in their being consigned to a
watery grave.—The piece, on the whole, is beautifully
pathetic.

EARL RICHARD'S DAUGHTER.
Page 142.

This ballad I have never seen before in any shape or dress.
It narrates the daughter of a wealthy Earl falling in love
with her kitchen boy, whom she sent to sea in a ship of her
own contriving. From his being closely besieged by a

Spanish lady of rank and fortune, to tender his love to her,
we may reasonably suppose he possessed that enchanting
air and mien which are so often the inroads to a female heart.
He, however, kept his integrity and vows inviolate, till he
arrived in his own country, where he was hailed by Earl
Richard as a personage of rank, and introduced as such to
his daughter ; when, under a mask, he delivered unto her
the ring that he had received at their parting.　After having
witnessed the tender emotions which filled her heart, and a
few fits of that mania which love engenders, he pulled off
the mask, and made himself known.　He was afterwards
married to the lady, and nine months after brought him a
son and heir.—The Earl Richard, the lady's father, is said
to have been one of the Earls of Wemyss.

There is such a striking and visible coincidence between
this hallad and Hynd Horn, that I am apt to think they are
coeval.

WILLIE AND LADY MAISRY.

Page 151.

This beautifully pathetic ballad will pave the way for the
reception of Clerk Sandy, to which it bears a great resemblance. It is indeed one of that class of ballads which
glistens the eyes of a nervous reader on its perusal.
Although Willie had been made to perform one of those deeds
which would stagger the belief even of the most ancient and
enthusiastic admirers of chivalry ; he is kept free from that
disgusting ribaldry of nonsense which is often made to ac-
company valorous actions in some of our old ballads.　His
fate every one will deplore ; for, although he had killed his
lover's brother, and thirty-two of her father's guards, it was
only in self-defence.

An imperfect copy of a ballad, on a similar subject, is to
be found in the Minstrelsy Ancient and Modern, p. 370,
taken down, as the editor says, "from the recitation of a
lady far advauced in years."

CLERK SANDY.

Page 156.

This ballad is one of the many that have undergone a trans-mutation, from its being handed down by oral tradition. As language and manners change, so does the voice of song ; every reciter considering himself warranted to substitute that which he knows to be no part of the work, to supply deficiencies. In many cases, that romantic age of chivalry is gone. The young knight does not now go in search of perilous adventures at tilts and tournaments, to make him-self acceptable to his fair enslaver. Honour, at one time, was the watch-word, but now seduction, Oh ! how are the mighty fallen !—Sir Walter Scott and Mr Jamieson have each preserved a copy in their several Collections, but both differ from this one. Sir Walter's copy concludes with the five last verses of " William's Ghost," published by Wother-spoon, vol. i. p. 76. Mr Jamieson's copy is still more anti-quated, but also composed of shreds and patches. In Mr J.'s copy, the hero is called an Earl's son ; the heroine, a king's daughter.

WILLIE AND FAIR BURD ANN.

Page 163.

This ballad recounts the love that existed between a faith-ful pair :—what the lady gave her lover to begin his fortune ; —how he returned to the house of her parents after he had traded, and likely gained another hundred pounds, and stole away his betrothed bride in a misty night ; of their dis-appointments at shipping, and faithfulness to each other during their separation.

THE ENCHANTED RING.

Page 164.

This ballad, like many of its predecessors, is founded on the visionary belief of a supernatural agency in a piece of

gold and pebble. Such an opinion had long presided over
the minds of the ancients, not only of the ignorant, but of
the learned. Reginald Scot, in his Discovery of Witchcraft,
gives a catalogue of "the vertues and qualities of sundrie
pretious stones," &c., of which the following is a part :—

"The excellent vertues and qualities of stones found, conceived, and tried by this art, is wonderfull. Howbeit many
things most false and fabulous are added vnto their true
effects, wherewith I thought good in part to trie the readers
patience and cunning withal. Aggat (they saie) hath vertue
against the bitting of scorpions or serpents. It is written
that it maketh a man eloquent, and procureth the fauour of
princes ; yea, that the fume thereof dooth turne awaie
tempests. Alectorious is a stone about the bignesse of a
beane, as cleere as the christall, taken out of a cocks bellie
which hath beene gelt or made a capon foure yeares. If it
be held in ones mouth, it asswageth thirst, it maketh the
husband to loue the wife, and the bearer inuincible : for
heereby *Milo* was said to ouercome his enemies. A craw-
pocke deliuereth from prison. Chelidonius is a stone taken
out of a swallowe, which cureth melancholie ; howbeit, some
authors saie, it is the hearbe whereby the swallowes recouer
the sight of their young, even if their eies be picked out
with an instrument. Geranities is taken out of a crane, and
draconites out of a dragon. But it is to be noted, that such
stones must be taken out of the bellies of the serpents, beasts,
or birds, (wherein they are) whiles they live ; otherwise,
they vanish awaie with the life, and so they reteine the
vertues of those starres vnder which they are. Amethysus
maketh a droouken man sober, and refreshed the wit. The
coral preserueth such as beare it from facination or bewitch-
ing, and in this respect they are hanged about children's
necks." He goes on to enumerate, I know not how many
more, which would but weary the patience of a sceptical
reader, and cause him think his time but mis-spent in the
perusal of such jargon.

BROOM O' THE COWDENKNOWES.
Page 167.

This beautiful old pastoral has been repeatedly published in mutilated parts; every editor giving his copy of it as the original. The very ashes of the dead, and all those who have gone before, have been harrowed up, and the spirits of departed antiquarians conjured from their rest by the poetical magician, to supply imaginary breaches. I have also contributed my mite to gratify the lovers of ancient song, by an edition, which, though last in publication, I hope is not least in poetical merit, among those that have already pleased so much. Like the hero of many of the other ballads, this one has been localized by different reciters, to suit their caprice or vanity, in ascribing to him the sovereignty of the places where they reside, as every person wishes to immortalize the place of his nativity or residence.

PROUD MAITLAND.
Page 175.

Whether this great personage be meant for Sir Richard Maitland of Lethington, a descendant of Auld Maitland's, of which so much has been said and sung; or Chancellor Maitland, who made so much noise in the time of King James VI., I am not quite certain. "We have already seen one instance," says Sir Walter Scott, in his note to "Auld Maitland;" "and in an elegant copy of verses in the Maitland MSS., in praise of Sir Richard's seat of Lethington, which he had built, or greatly improved, this obvious topic of flattery does not escape the poet. From the terms of his panegyric we learn, that the exploits of Auld Sir Richard with the grey beard, and of his three sons, were 'sung in many far countrie, albeit in rural rhyme;' from which we may infer, that they were narrated rather in the shape of a popular ballad, than a *romance of price.* If this be the case, the song now published may have undergone little variation since the date of the Maitland MSS.; for, divesting the poem, in praise of Leth-

ington, of its antique spelling, it would run as smoothly, and
appear as modern, as any verse in the following ballad. The
lines alluded to, arc addressed to the castle of Lethington."

This is the first and only time I have ever seen this ballad,
either MS. or printed.

LORD DARLINGTON.

Page 178.

In Joseph Ritson's Northumbrian Ballads, there is one
called "Fair Mabel of Wallington," which has some simi-
larity to the present.

The young ladies, according to Calvin's doctrine, had been
predestinated ere they were born to die in child-bed, and
that nothing could have saved them, as the decree had once
gone forth. The unfortunate lady, the last of the sisters, was
of the house of Seaton, Aberdeenshire.

BLUE FLOWERS AND YELLOW.

Page 181.

It may be said of Willie, as was said of Sir James the Rose,
that,—

> "Lang had he woo'd, lang she refused,
>   In seeming scorn and pride ;
> Yet aft her eyes confess'd the love,
>   Her fearful words deny'd ;"

till his father, a wylie old churl, proposed a novel stratagem
to prove her love, and to get her entangled in a snare prepared for her. It was no less successful than curious ; it had
the desired effect, and Willie gained his heart's desire.

JEAN O' BETHELNIE'S LOVE FOR SIR GEORGE GORDON.

Page 184.

When the intestine troubles and broils of the North dis-
turbed the public peace so much, in 1562, the Queen's

presence was thought necessary to put a stop to some of them ; and for that purpose she appeared in the North among her friends and foes. Jean, daughter of Baron Meldrum, and Laird of Bethelnie, in Aberdeenshire, was one of Queen Mary's favourites, with whom she occasionally dined at the house of Fetternear, where the Queen resided for a few days ; and having chanced to espy Sir George Gordon of Glenlogie, as he rode through the village of Banchory, fell desperately in love with him ; and, that he might know her case, she despatched a letter to him for the purpose ; but he, for a while, made light of the same, which came to the lady's ears, and threw her into a violent fever. Her father's chaplain, no doubt bred at the court of Cupid, undertook the correspondence, and was more successful. She was shortly afterward married to Sir George, the object of her wishes, in her fifteenth year.

THE HOLY NUNNERY.
Page 188.

A nunnery is a sort of religious house, or receptacle for virgins who have bound themselves by a vow to live a single and chaste life,—celibacy being accounted honourable. There are few, I presume, but have read the unfortunate fate of Abelard and Eloise : how they were disappointed in their early loves, and spent their latter days in a monastery. Such was the case with the unfortunate pair in this ballad ; for, at one time, nunneries were common in Scotland, endowed with extraordinary privileges. Many fabulous but amusing stories, and lively anecdotes, have been told of the nuns who have taken the veil, &c. In the Island of Iona, or Icolmkill, the dilapidated ruins of an Augustinian nunnery are still to be seen. The church is 58 feet by 20 on the floor, and contains the tomb of the last prioress, though now considerably defaced. The figure is carved, praying to the Virgin Mary, with the address under her feet : *Sancta Maria, ora pro me*, and with this inscription round the ledge, in old British characters : *Hic jacet Domina Anna Donaldi Ferleti filia, quondam prioressa de Iona, quæ*

obiit, anno MDXI. cujus animam (altissimo) commendamus.
At the first establishment of the monastery, the nuns resided
on a small isle near I., still called the Isle of Nuns. Columba,
at length, relented so far, as to allow them this establishment
on the island, where they wore a white gown, and over
it a rocket of white linen.

THE NEW SLAIN KNIGHT.
Page 193.

It was, at one time, quite a common thing for two lovers to
make trial of each other's affections, unknown to one another ;
which, if they found to vibrate according to the notes of their
own hearts and feelings, they were rewarded accordingly.
Under the mask of a stranger, did the hero of this ballad try
his lady's love, and found it sincere.

THE WHITE FISHER.
Page 195.

Those who have read the lives of the Popes ; the history of
the inquisition, and of the inferior orders of the clergy of the
Romish church, will be nowise surprised that the ghostly
confessor should, instead of administering spiritual consolation
to the lady in her husband's absence, rob her of her chastity ;
and betray, like an unprincipled villain, the trust reposed in
him. The wicked lives and ungrateful conduct of most of the
friars, monks, and priests, need no comment. It would appear
from the indulgence given to the lady by her husband, that he
was conscious of the priest's treachery, and of her own innocence, in as far as she was betrayed.

LORD DINGWALL.
Page 199.

This ballad has all the insignia of antiquity stamped upon
it ; and records one of those romantic fashions said to exist in
the Highlands of Scotland some hundred years ago. I am not

inclined to think that the hero of the piece was any of the Lords Dingwall, although its name would imply as much ; but rather a Highland chieftain, or Laird of Dingwall, a royal borough in Ross-shire; if such be the real name of the ballad; of which I am dubious, for Sir Richard Preston was created Lord Dingwall by King James in 1607, by patent, to the heirs of his body. His only daughter and heir, Lady Elizabeth, married James, the great Duke of Ormond. His grandson, James second and last Duke, claimed, in 1710, the Scotch honour of Dingwall ; for which he was allowed to vote at the election of the sixteen peers the same year. This title was forfeited by his attainder, in 1715. From this we may see, that none of the Lords of Dingwall resided in the Highlands, but most part in England, which confirms my opinion.

In an imperfect copy of a ballad somewhat similar in incident to this one, the hero of the piece is called "Lord Bothwell ; " but which of the two is the true title, I am not determined to say.

JAMES HERRIES.
Page 209.

Sir Walter Scott has given a ballad under the designation of the "Dæmon Lover," vol. ii. p. 427, of the Border Min- strelsy, which he says was taken down from recitation by Mr William Laidlaw. In this ballad, a few of the incidents are narrated ; but it wants all the particulars which render it either perfect, or complete. In the Minstrelsy Ancient and Modern, is a fragment given, all that could be procured by the indefatigable editor of that work. I am therefore happy to say, I have it now in my power to convince my esteemed friend, there is still a *perfect* copy of this curious and scarce legend in existence, which is now, for the first time, given to the public. In this ballad, it is not a demon or fiend, that betrays Jeannie Douglas, but the spirit of her own first true love, James Herries, who had died abroad, but now come to punish her for perjury, infidelity, and to recover from her the pledges of her broken vows.

James Herries was a branch of the Anglo-Norman family
of Heriz, who came into Scotland during the age of David.
It is more than probable, that the same William de Heriz,
who appears to have attached himself to David I., and his
son Henry, may have settled in Scotland.   The representa-
tive of all those Herizes, Sir Herbert, obtained the title of
Lord Herries of Terregles in 1493.   From this stock are
sprung the several families of Herris in Scotland.—*Caledonia.*

BARBARA BLAIR.
Page 213.

Barbara Blair is the young woman's name who had fallen
in love with a sea captain, to whom she was with child, and
was ardently attached, much against her mother's inclination,
who wished him drowned in the sea.   The captain, however,
proved a man of honour, and repaired the breach which he
had made in the young woman's character, by his speedily
marrying her, which made the old woman change her song.

THOMAS O' YONDERDALE.
Page 216.

This beautiful ballad I do not recollect of having seen anywhere else.   Thomas makes love to Lady Maisry, and gains
what had been often attempted in vain by many rich and
noble suitors, the heart of the young lady.   He had, however, no sooner deprived her of her innocence, than he left
her and her helpless off-spring, in a hopeless and forlorn
condition.   He went to England ; continued in that country
for some time, and wooed another bride for to bring home,
but was chid for his inconstancy by Lady Maisry, who stood
by his bed-side one night in a dream.   This pricked him to
the heart, and caused him return with all the haste he may,
to the land which he had left, and marry the first object of
his love, and leave his English betrothed bride to go maiden
home.

THE KNIGHT'S GHOST.

Page 221.

Dunfermline has the honour of being celebrated in many of our old Scottish songs; and was once the scene of much mirth and merriment; at other times, bustle and strife. It was here where many of the Scottish kings spent much of their time, and administered justice to their subjects. It was here where the remains of the valiant and renowned Robert Bruce were deposited; and it was here where the good lady lost her husband, surrounded by his faithful band of mariners, fighting for his life to their knees in blood. If we take it, from the authority of this ballad, that the souls of the departed are privy to all that is passing in this lower world, we are not only informed of the past, but also made to believe they have a prescience, or foreknowledge of what will follow. This ghost was a generous and liberal one in many respects.

THE TROOPER AND FAIR MAID.

Page 224.

This is not the first "bonny lass that has lien in a barrack, followed a sodger, and carried his wallet." In this ballad will be found the identical lines which gave so much room for critical acumen among the poetical antiquaries of the last century, regarding "Waly, Waly up the bank," in which some mistaken editors have maintained that they should have been inserted, as belonging to that song. The Trooper and Fair Maid was written prior to Waly, Waly up the bank.

LORD INGRAM AND CHILDE VYET.

Page 227.

A ballad somewhat similar to this one appeared in Mr Jamieson's Popular Ballads, vol. ii. p. 265, as taken from Herd's MSS.; but it is deficient in many respects, when compared with the present complete copy; particularly in that which gives it the pathos and sublimity. I have also seen another copy, but still it had its defects. The ballad records the fate of two brothers who had made love to one lady; their tragic end, with the lady's penitence.

CASTLE HA'S DAUGHTER.
Page 235.

Another ballad of a similar description, called Bold Burnett's Daughter, I took down about the same time as the present one, from a different person; but as it is so much alike in manner and incident, I have, for the present, withheld it. There are various ballads to be met with of the same nature, which rather than please, shock humanity. Every thing of a preposterous and absurd imagination served as food for the Doric muse, and inspired it with antediluvian vigour.

WILLIE'S DROWNED IN GAMERY.
Page 239.

The unfortunate hero of this ballad, was a factor to the laird of Kinmundy. As the young woman to whom he was to be united in connubial wedlock resided in Gamery, a small fishing town on the east coast of the Murray Frith, the marriage was to be solemnized in the church of that parish, to which he was on his way, when overtaken by some of the heavy breakers which overflow a part of the road he had to pass, and dash, with impetuous fury, against the lofty and adamantine rocks with which it is skirted. The young damsel, in her fifteenth year, also met with a watery grave, being the wages of her mother's malison. This ballad will remind the reader of the Drowned Lovers, who shared the same fate in the river Clyde.

LANG JOHNNY MOIR.
Page 242.

This ballad I never saw anywhere else, in one shape nor

another ; but am informed it is very old, having been written about the time of King Robert Bruce, as the characters that are introduced into it, assisted at the siege of Carlisle. It is undoubtedly of a political nature. The gigantic statures of Johnny and his relations are such as would stagger the belief even of those enthusiasts who are well acquainted with the traditions and fairy fictions of Benachie, the place to which Johnny belonged, in Aberdeenshire. Such fabulous relations of men and things, often embellish the ballads of the ancients, partly from conviction and partly from ignorance. The place where Johnny resided was at Hartshill, and his uncle at a place called the Beech. John o' Noth was the proprietor of Noth, a great hill, from its high conical summit commonly called the top of Noth ; on which, overlooking an immense track of country, are the remains of an ancient fortress, formerly thought to have been the mouth of a volcano, but now known to be one of those forts constructed of stones vitrified by the force of fire, of which kind many have been lately discovered in Scotland. In the parish of Auchindoir, to which Johnny belonged, a little below Craig, stood the Castrum Auchindores, mentioned by Buchanan, under the reign of James II., the remains of which are still visible.

CUTTIE'S WEDDING.
Page 250.

The music and words of this song were composed by a Mr Smith, who followed, as a musician, the variegated fortunes of the late pretender, Prince Charles Edward Stewart, at Culloden, and many other places. He at length settled in Peterhead as a violin player, upon which instrument he excelled. The wedding took place at a small ale-house in a fishing village called Drum Lithe, parish of St Fergus, about sixty years ago ; being what was called a siller or penny wedding. Cuttie was the nickname of the bridegroom, who was a fisherman ; and, to this day, a small rivulet that passed his house retains the name of "Cuttie's Burn"—his name and family, in other respects, are extinct. I have heard of an old woman

called "Cuddie," who has also been immortalized by some
kind poet in four lines, which run thus :—

> There was an auld wife, they ca'd her Cuddie,
> And a' body said she wou'd gang to the wuddie;
> But yet she die't wi' a better commend,
> For she danc'd hersell dead at her ain hous end !

MISS GORDON OF GIGHT.
Page 251.

I need not say, the following song, has been written by a
Scottish bard, who had been dissatisfied with the marriage of
Miss Gordon of Gight to John Byron, son of Admiral Byron.
They were father and mother of the late much lamented but
immortal Lord Byron.

THE LITTLE MAN.
Page 256.

A ballad somewhat similar in name and circumstances, is
to be found in some old Collections of Ballads ; but this is the
only genuine copy with which I ever met.   The scene of the
meeting is in the Garioch, at the foot of Benachie, a high
mountain in Aberdeenshire ; a place long and justly celebrated
for the nocturnal visits of the Elfin train, to which this romantic ballad seems to relate.

THE POOR AULD MAIDENS.
Page 258.

This curious ditty was written during the sovereignty of
James the Third, King of Scotland, and consequently nearly
four hundred years old.

THE GUISE OF TYRIE.
Page 260.

The hero of this curious song was the Reverend Mr Andrew
Cant, a character much celebrated in the history of the

troubles of Scotland in the seventeenth century. His induct-
ment to the pastoral charge of the parish of Tyrie, of which
he was the first Protestant minister, having given great offence
to the rabble, one of them composed the Guise of Tyrie. Mr
Cant being an avowed enemy to all, and everything that
savoured of Popery, being boarded in the house of Mr Forbes,
the proprietor of Boyndlie, who was a Papist, in his bed-room
were hung a great many of the Saints' pictures. Having an
aversion to these, he requested that they might be taken
down. The laird, to please his guest, took down St Peter,
and hung up the picture of Mr Cant, with these lines written
underneath :

> Come down, St Peter,
> Ye superstitious saint,
> And let up your better—
> Mr Andrew Cant.

THE FAUSE LOVER.

Page 261.

In all the printed Collections of Old Ballads I have as yet
consulted, I have found great deficiencies, such as giving
mutilated fragments for complete copies, which I have endeavoured, as much as possible, to avoid. The only eight lines
of this ballad I have ever met with in print were published by
Mr Herd.

ROBYN'S TESMENT.

Page 265.

This little piece, I am convinced, is very old, as its style and
language, although modernized, will testify. I have every
reason to think it has been composed under the cloud of disguise, upon some great family, and on some particular event,
though now unknown ; as was the ballad of the " *Wren*,"
composed on Lord Lennox's love to a daughter of Lord
Blantyre's.

RICHARD'S MARY.

Page 267.

Mary Mortimer was the name of this lady, who was a staunch Papist in the Enzie. When her husband died, she spent all her living on priests in praying him out of purgatory, whence his spirit had gone for the purification of his soul.

THE CUNNING CLERK.

Page 270.

This humorous ballad is local, but very old. Collieston, where the scene is laid, is a small fishing town on the east coast of Aberdeenshire, once so justly famed as being the rendezvous of Dutch and Flushing smugglers. That spirit with which the ballad commences is kept up through the whole with great naivete and eclat. It belongs to a class rarely to be met with. I never saw any one in print bear the smallest resemblance to it. My worthy friend in Paisley was kind enough as to send me a copy of one somewhat similar in incident, as taken down from the recitation of an old woman in that quarter.

Clerks are often introduced to the notice of the public, by the old rhymesters, in their antiquated ballads : but we are not now to suppose them to be journeymen shopkeepers, accountants, lawyers' assistants, *alias* scribes, nor book-keepers, but journeymen priests, who were wont to do the drudgery of the higher orders of the Romish church, and were a class of men well skilled in the art of debauchery, &c.

THE CLERKS OF OXENFORD.

Page 273.

These young gentlemen were the sons of the Laird of Oxenford, who had given them a part of all the education that that place of the country could boast, and afterwards were sent to Billsbury, a famous town at that time celebrated for its seminaries of learning. Here the young men, although particularly warned of the danger, and advised not to come too near the persons of the mayor's daughters, forgot their parents' injunction at parting, and became enamoured of the young women, which reached the mayor's ears, and proved their destiny. Although their lives had been requested by their father, and also by their lovers, the mayor's daughters, he caused them both to be hanged.—This must have been in the time of the feudal law.

END OF THE FIRST VOLUME.

TURNBULL AND SPEARS, PRINTERS, EDINBURGH.

www.ingramcontent.com/pod-product-compliance
Lightning Source LLC
Chambersburg PA
CBHW020934030726
47496CB00005B/1179